MORE DEAD THAN ALIVE

Surely there could be no possibility that Konrad Klein could be alive—no one could be expected to have left by the turret window and survive. With the door blocked and the window wide open, surely it had to be suicide? But Konrad was a leading illusionist and one-time escapologist, so there must be some doubt even though he was on the verge of a breakdown. Kilvennan Castle is shaken by deceptions and emotional conflicts before answers are found.

MORE DEAD THAN ALIVE

Roger Ormerod

BLACK DAGGER CRIME

First published 1980
by
Robert Hale Ltd

This edition 2004 by BBC Audiobooks Ltd
published by arrangement with
the author

ISBN 1 4056 8503 4

British Library Cataloguing in Publication Data available

Printed and bound in Great Britain by
Antony Rowe Ltd., Chippenham, Wiltshire

AUTHOR'S NOTE

I feel I should apologise to the Magic Circle for introducing two illusions without reference to their archives. But I am sure I would have been told that the one was not possible to stage, and the other I have invented purely for the purposes of my story, and was never intended to stage.

Needless to say, any reference to persons living or dead is not intended, but partly in reparation this book is dedicated to the Magic Circle, in memory of so many splendid illusions that have baffled me and given me pleasure, and have worked so much better than mine.

R.O.

ONE

I always worry when David is late. He'd said he would come straight away, which, in that Porsche of his, would have meant three hours for the 160 miles, even cross-country. But he was late.

Eventually I found myself on the battlements, my back to the racing sea-wind, looking out over the wide and falling valley, over the woodland to the grey horizon, watching the ribbon of winding road which appeared in loops between the trees. And when I finally saw the lone car it was not the Porsche, but George's.

I was not certain whether I was pleased. I have a deep affection for David's partner, George, but Clarice had asked simply for advice, and now, with the full manpower of their detective agency on the way, it made the whole thing something more like a case.

I was relieved to be able to turn away, although my return journey meant facing the wind and walking towards the High Tower, with all its menace, and closer to the sullen roar and surge of the sea against the cliffs. During the early days of my visit I had been pleasantly awed by the grandeur; now it filled me with dread. I hurried to the small door in the lea of the tower, and shut it away from me. The walls were three feet of solid stone, but although I could no longer hear it I believed that I could still feel the throb of the sea.

The steep stone staircase led down to another door on to the Long Gallery. I walked down the Grand Staircase and into the Great Hall. Everywhere in Kilvennan Castle bore capitals and an adjective. I found Clarice in the Cleric's library.

"They're coming," I said.

"They?"

I had not noticed Anthony, sitting almost hidden in a high-backed easy chair across the fire from his stepmother. I did not know that Clarice had told him of her request to me—nearer a plea perhaps. "My husband and his partner," I told him.

He grimaced. Anthony had a long, mobile face on which a grimace could explore all the emotions from distaste to cynical amusement. I felt no attachment for Anthony. He was a year or two younger than me—put him at 26—but his self-assurance was of a much more mature man. He carried his six feet lithely, and I have no doubt looked very sleek in his stage costume of white tie and tails. But I did not trust his hands.

Clarice was looking distressed. Perhaps she had been arguing, yet again, with Anthony. I hoped it was not my announcement that had upset her.

"You'll like George Coe," I assured her. "Between them, they'll sort it out."

"Hah!" said Anthony in disgust. "What's the matter with the police? Why can't we wait for the inquest verdict?"

"Oh . . . really!" Clarice was annoyed, though it was obvious he was deliberately baiting her. She flashed me a brief appeal with those wide, grey eyes of hers. I didn't know what she expected. I was not even sure what her obvious lack of mourning was intended to mean; perhaps a deliberate affront to Anthony. And yet, she had surely loved her husband, and I was sure Anthony had hated him.

"There must be a few details to clarify," I said gently. "David could well produce evidence for the inquest."

He played with a coin, riffling it along the knuckles of his right hand until it vanished, to appear and perform again along his left. He glanced up at me.

"We'll see, Elsa, we'll see."

I was relieved to hear the car drawing up outside. The side window of this room looked out on the wide, gravel sweep of the drive below the stepped terrace. I went across and saw George climb out, look round him appraisingly, and say something to David as they stood together. David looked solemn, perhaps a little disturbed by the castle, as I had been at first. It really was rather overpowering. I went out into the Hall to let them in.

Having considered the question, I had come to the conclusion that it had been quite reasonable for a man like Konrad Klein to buy such a property. It was broken down, had ancient plumbing and facilities, was cold and draughty and inconvenient, but its massive flamboyance had exactly matched his personality. It had a dour and mysterious aura about it, especially in moonlight when the bats sailed over the battlements and the barn owls cried in the night. This had been the natural habitat for such a man.

But the residual finances had not run to more help than a cook-housekeeper and a chauffeur-gardener, so that I had to open the huge doors myself, and say: "David, you're late."

Then Clarice was at my shoulder, making the correct social noises, and George was hugging me and banging his cheek on mine, as though I hadn't seen him only a month before.

"Elsa, you look marvellous. Doesn't she, Dave?"

"Always," said David loyally, kissing me gently, absent-mindedly. He turned to Clarice, taking her hand, smiling. "I hear you have a problem, Mrs Klein."

"Clarice," she murmured. "Elsa and I were friends at school, so we must be friends too." She eyed George doubtfully—he's so big and generally untidy. "And . . . George, is it? . . George, too."

David and George agreed readily enough, each apparently anxious to complete the formalities and get me alone. She appeared to realise this. "Elsa will show you your room, David, of course. But you, George, I must admit you've caught me on the wrong foot. I'll have to put you next to Elsa and David, but the bed isn't made up. Perhaps you'd care to . . ." She made a vague gesture towards the Library, but Anthony was lounging in the doorway, cynical eyebrows raised, waiting for an introduction, and, I thought, poised to turn away if it was offered.

"We'll just go up to our room," I suggested, to her obvious relief.

I led the way up the Grand Staircase, with George carrying all their baggage and David absent-mindedly filling his pipe. "Looks like a set for a Dracula film," said David, and George added: "Wouldn't like to pay the rates."

They did not know, at that time, that most of the rooms were empty and musty, and parts of the structure collapsing. The electricity system depended on a diesel-powered dynamo somewhere across the courtyard, and was ancient. Dracula would have demanded more comfort.

"In here," I said.

All the doors were deep-set, heavy oak, with latches but no locks. The room itself was high and deep, the windows looking out over the courtyard, narrow and tall windows, uncurtained. The furnishings were adze-chipped from black oak, from the quaint stool in front of my hand-carved dressing-table to the immense wardrobe. The bed would have slept all three of us. It did not even creak when George flopped his great weight on it.

"Now," said David, leaning back against the door, "what *is* all this, Elsa?"

"I did tell you on the phone, David. Konrad is dead—he must be—and the suggestion is that it was suicide."

"Whose suggestion?" asked George.

"The police. This happened a week ago. And naturally, losing her husband, and the police . . . Clarice is distressed."

"That he's dead?" David asked. "Or that it was suicide?"

And George said: "She didn't seem upset to me."

Looking back to our schooldays, our period at finishing school in Switzerland when Clarice had been head prefect, I must admit that she had never seemed distressed. Clarice, come to think of it, would never allow herself to be unduly disturbed by outside influences; she influenced them.

"She doesn't show her feelings. But I know she's upset. It was so . . . dreadful, you see. Konrad was in his workroom—he called it his laboratory—up in the Tower. It overlooks the sea and the cliffs—I'll show you later—and he was working on one of his cabinets. From here—from this room—because I had the window open, and I suppose because he had his open, I heard the shot . . ."

"Shot?" said George with interest. But David made a slight gesture, and George was silent.

"There were always shots," I told them. "It was part of what he was doing with that cabinet of his. So I didn't take much notice of just a shot, but then there was this loud crash. I suppose it echoed right down the Tower, because even Clarice heard it, and she was in the Pink Lounge. And the crash wasn't usual. So I ran out, and Clarice was hurrying up the stairs to the gallery, so we went into the Tower together. It's right near the top—oh, there's hundreds of stairs. When we got to the door we were quite breathless. Anyway, she banged on the door. It's like this one, thick and heavy. You don't get much of a sound, but of course it wasn't locked and she turned the latch but the door wouldn't budge. Not an inch. We both pushed at it, but there's not much room for two to stand, and we couldn't move it. And there was no sound from inside. I tell you, I was getting quite scared. Clarice said, 'Rush down and get somebody—one of the men,' so I started down those wretched steps, and met Anthony coming up. You saw him, hanging around in that doorway like a disapproving cloud."

They nodded solemnly, though I thought George was suppressing a smile. I hurried on.

"You can be sure Anthony was taking his time. For his father he wasn't going to put himself out. I turned back up those stairs again and he followed me, not a bit out of breath, and when we got to the door he just said give him room, all lazily confident you know, and he had a go at it himself, got his shoulder right down to it, turned the latch up, and put all his strength behind it. And it opened slowly—you could hear the dragging sound—but in the end he had it open enough to get in. The cabinet had been lying on its back against the door, and he'd had to slide it away."

"And this Konrad had shot himself," said George.

"Oh, no. Not at all. He just wasn't there, and the window, right opposite the door, that was wide open, so that . . . well, he couldn't have gone anywhere else, and when you see it—the fall to the rocks . . . Oh, David, he *must* be dead."

"Doubtless," said David negligently, but he had that look in his eyes, that inward peering awareness, which indicated he was keenly interested. "So why send for us, Elsa?"

I glanced at George, not wishing to remind them that I'd sent for David alone. "It's kind of . . . well, Clarice was saying, it was one of Konrad's little, cold jokes, that he'd be worth more dead than alive . . ."

David said smoothly: "And is he?"

"You won't believe the insurance he took out, David. But of course it was partly professional advertisement, and all of it would be non-payable if he committed suicide. So you see . . ."

I looked from one to the other. They did not fully appreciate the situation. Their faces were blank and unresponsive.

"But surely you've realised! Konrad Klein was the greatest escapologist since Houdini, and one of the world's leading illusionists. His stage name was Konrad Klimax."

Obsessed with the letter K, he had been. I supposed that even the K of Kilvennan had attracted him. Given time he'd have been spelling his home as Kastle. It was his talisman, K, as in kunning and kold. I hadn't liked him, but Clarice was my friend.

"Clarice is my friend!" I said angrily when they looked uneasy and glanced at each other. "David, she can't accept that he committed suicide."

"Of course she would not."

"You don't have to sound so bitter, David."

"Ask yourself. Are you expecting us to prove it wasn't suicide, for the sake of . . . how many thousands! Elsa?"

"Oh, you're being so stupid. Both of you. Would such a man, even if he intended to take his own life, do it in such a way that it was obvious? When he'd boasted about being worth so much dead! No, of course he wouldn't. He'd at least create an illusion that it wasn't suicide. It was his career, David. Do you imagine he couldn't create one grand, final illusion, if only to disguise his suicide as . . . something else?"

"Easy, love, easy," said David. "There's something in what you say. But obviously he didn't, because that's what it looks like."

I can't always be patient with him. "Then don't you think you ought to find out why?"

George levered himself to his feet and stretched. "Perhaps he wasn't given any choice."

"Oh, come on, George." David sounded irritable. "With that cabinet against the door?"

"Well, let's go and see this wonderful room."

"Later," said David. "Do we get to eat, Elsa?"

"Dinner's in . . . ten minutes. Time for a wash and a clean shirt. We'll go up afterwards."

George was at the door, invigorated by the mention of food. David seemed to catch him with his tone. "It's not what we usually do, helping a widow fiddle the insurance company."

"It's not like that!"

"Isn't it, Elsa? Perhaps that's what we ought to clear up first."

"After we eat," said George.

"You'll see," I assured them, "*while* we eat. You'll meet them all."

TWO

They used a corner of the old ballroom as a dining recess, the real dining-room having deposited its ceiling on the floor. We went down together. David and I were informal, he in slacks and that splendid cashmere cardigan Doris bought him for Christmas. George had put on his other suit, the one with the narrow lapels and the waistcoat, and looked massively complacent.

Clarice was already there, fussing with the table settings as though her arrangements could be anything but perfect, and to my surprise, because she always seems to be last in everything, Amaryllis Moore was standing against the carved stone mantel, smoking a cigarette. But of course, she was always eager to see a fresh male face; twice as eager for two.

I introduced them. George beamed, much taken, and David was gravely attentive, which told me how attractive he found her.

"Amaryllis?" he asked. "Very unusual."

"It's Amanda, really. But for the stage Amaryllis is more catching."

David glanced at me, raising his eyebrows. And to think I hadn't told him!

She was considering him seriously with those huge, brown eyes of hers, which gained so much from her fine-boned face with the high cheekbones, and her pert little pixie mouth. She poised the combined result on a long neck from what I'd have called bony shoulders. But then, she'd had no end of poising practice. Her whole body spoke of it, her lithe collectedness and her long, slim and supple limbs.

"Amaryllis was a ballet dancer," I explained, before David had explored all the possibilities.

"But not recently," she told him, in case he expected her to go up on to her points. "For the last five years I've worked with Konrad."

"His assistant," I said.

She flashed me a look of distaste. "Partner," she purred. "His partner. He said I had the right body for it."

George said: "The table's laid for eight," and when she tried the same look on him he beamed at her. "The right body for sawing in half?" he asked.

"Konrad's illusions were a little more advanced than that." She was very cool with him.

I had not noticed Anthony, quietly walking the full length of the ballroom. One doesn't; he simply appears. Now, hearing the last remark, he interrupted with restrained savagery, his voice smooth and low-pitched.

"My father was on the way out before he met you, my dear. Who wants full-stage illusions these days? He couldn't get near a theatre stage in the past two years, and illusions are dead on television because you always half believe it's a trick of the camera. But we're all happy to have you with us, of course. Aren't we, Clarice?" He paused. Clarice had turned, frowning, obviously unsure, as I was, whether he was denigrating his father or Amaryllis. She made no reply, knowing it was simply a dramatic pause. Anthony swept a hand in grave acknowledgement. "Amaryllis, darling, you at least kept him sane, right to the end."

If he was deliberately trying to disturb her poise he was far from succeeding. It was too professional. "Dear Anthony," she murmured, and Clarice was looking rapidly from David to George, assessing the damage this might have wrought in their opinions.

But George was bland, and David simply turned to me, took my arm and said softly: "Did you notice the Copley? I'm sure its genuine."

"Nothing," claimed Anthony in facetious triumph, "in this damned place is genuine, except the bloody stone walls."

"Eight places," said George again, impatient to get at the food. "Who're we waiting for?"

They came in together, Martin Fisher and Auden Sundry, almost arm in arm. I'd rarely seen them apart, but they were old friends, as Fisher's company handled all the insurance cover for the Magic Circle, and Sundry was their President.

"Let me introduce you," I said, and when I had done so we moved to our places.

I was not deceived by George's immediate absorption with the food, which was served by Clarice's cook-housekeeper. George always has an ear cocked. I spoke occasionally to Martin Fisher, on my left, because he's the bouncy sort who will not allow you to remain uninvolved, but my attention was mainly for David, who was demanding facts, facts, facts . . .

"The funny little man on my left is in insurance," I explained. "Naturally, he's here. No . . . listen, David, there's been no claim—it's too soon. He was here before. He'd have to be, because of the huge cover they gave Konrad on his illusions. He was here to see the new one, and decide whether it was too dangerous."

David smiled across the table at Clarice and said, not looking at me: "Dangerous? Surely not. That's one of the points of the thing—to look dangerous, kind of breathtaking. But there's never any real danger."

And Auden Sundry took him up on that, as I suppose he'd have to. "Oh, but I assure you, there's sometimes very real danger. Don't you remember Chung Fu Li, who used to catch bullets in his teeth?"

George lifted an eyebrow, fork poised. "Catch them?"

Something in his tone cut through the general chatter. There was a sudden silence. I saw Anthony rest his hand on Amaryllis's on the table. She did not withdraw it. Sundry seized on the pause, plunging in, laughing.

"My dear sir, don't sound so incredulous. Of course it was an illusion. Yet one evening he failed and was shot dead on the stage." There was a murmur of protest. He basked in the sensation. "It was never explained, because nobody ever knew how the illusion was done, because he hadn't filed details in our archives. But certainly he died."

"And cost my company a cool 50 thou," cut in

Fisher. "Before my time, mind you. But it's a legend at Head Office. These people cover themselves heavily to allow for accidents during the performance—or rehearsal. Pure theatrical publicity . . ."

"Oh, I can't accept that," Sundry protested, but amused.

"No? Then why do they bill themselves, these escapologists, as the man they won't insure."

"And why," demanded Sundry, "do *you* insure them, and quietly collect the premiums—and make damn sure they're safe before you offer your fabled double-indemnity? Now *that's* what I call publicity."

But they were teasing each other, along the length of the table. Clarice, aware that her dinner was proceeding smoothly, was smiling quietly to herself. David cleared his throat.

"And that's what Konrad Klein had, was it, double-indemnity?"

Martin Fisher was fractionally cool. "I'd countersigned the policy."

"So it wasn't dangerous, this thing of his?"

"Of course it was dangerous," said Amaryllis sharply. "I warned him . . ."

"Warned?" said David gently. "Were you expecting something to happen?"

She moved her head impatiently. The sweet was being served. George was patting his lips with his napkin, looking interested.

"Not," put in Anthony, "what did happen, I'm sure."

But she looked at him angrily, not welcoming his support. He saw it, and was momentarily hesitant. Then he recovered.

"Though I did expect something." He looked round the table. "I think we all did. All except dear, loyal

Amaryllis, who couldn't see he was finished, that this new cabinet of his was a failure, and that he was going totally and steadily insane." He looked up at the housekeeper. "None for me, thank you." And reached for his cigarettes.

There was a shocked silence at this calmly vicious outburst, and Clarice bent her head, one hand going up to cover her face. Beside me Fisher was nodding, nodding. He had to agree, was pleased to, but I could feel that he was tense with dislike. Beyond David, Sundry took it up with dignity. I had a tendency to forget that he, too, would no doubt be considered past it—in his sixties now. He was probably slowing; if speed was all. But the French word for conjuring says it better—legerdemain, meaning the speed of the hand. But now Sundry became the President for a few moments, gained vastly in dignity and stature, and calmly levelled a reprimand at Anthony.

"Nobody who matters ever considered your father as a failure, Anthony. The Magic Circle held him in great respect, or why would they ask me to be here, as their observer, when he gave his first showing?"

Anthony reacted to the dignity. "And you, sir, how did you react to father's corny old cabinet trick? Lord, you must all be bored to tears with vanishing cabinets, in all their variations. Shut somebody inside, slide in a few swords . . . What ability or technique does that need? It's all in the cabinet—"

"Swords!" said Sundry sharply. "But he was using bullets."

"Really!" Fisher protested. "You make me feel so . . . so hasty."

"In signing the policy?" asked David with interest.

But Fisher had intended it as a humorous diversion. He bobbed happily. "I'd got complete confidence in it.

I'd have gone in myself if it'd been twice as wide."

I had seen the cabinet, barely 18 inches square. Fisher had a 42 waist. We all laughed. Well, nearly all. George was looking unhappy.

The small diversion had distracted the attention from Clarice, which had obviously been Fisher's intention. He acted the part of the jolly buffoon, but more than once I had discovered him using remarkable sensitivity. I sneaked a look at her. Clarice was patting the corners of her eyes with a tiny handkerchief and trying to smile. When she spoke it was quietly, but at once she had the full attention of the whole table.

"Martin is very kind," she murmured. "But it does suit him—or his company, anyway—to believe that Konrad took his own life. No . . . no protests, Martin, please. It's part of your job, and we all understand. But Auden will tell you that poor Konrad, though he might have been close to a breakdown, was far too . . . too self-assured to take his own life." She glanced down. The next words were painful for her. "He was too proud to destroy what he considered to be one of God's perfect creations . . . himself."

Anthony burst in: "He was a bloody—" But Amaryllis rested the prongs of her fork on the back of his hand, and he gasped to silence.

"And," went on Clarice, "he was too professional not to have committed suicide in such a way that it would appear as something else . . ."

She blinked. David touched my arm. It was almost exactly what I had said myself.

"So . . . what do you believe?" he asked gently.

"I believe there was an accident."

"Involving this cabinet of his?"

"Yes."

Beside me Martin Fisher moved uneasily. "If you'll excuse me, Clarice, it's what you'd prefer *me* to believe." He looked round the table. "The cabinet was against the inside of the door. Konrad was an honourable man. It's just what he *would* do, if he'd intended to take his own life, just to make it clear that no one else could have been involved."

Clarice was shaking her head stubbornly. "An accident."

David breathed in my ear: "The double-indemnity clause."

"No, David!"

And George's eyes were on me, cynical and amused. Then he spoke with heavy politeness to Clarice. "You're saying that he'd fake a suicide as accident, just so that a fraud could be committed on the insurance company. We've heard that he was proud and honourable, but when it comes to it he was capable of being a cheat and a crook . . ."

"No," she whispered, choking.

"It was what you ruddy well said," he claimed, looking round for support. "That's how I heard it. And just because it looks like suicide you're asking us to accept that he didn't get round to using his natural deception—and so it must have been something else."

Clarice was staring at me with pain, accusing me of inflicting this ungracious and unsubtle man on her. I met her eyes, almost flinching.

"It's what you said, Clarice," I told her. "His life had become so involved with deliberate illusion—which is really fraud when you come to think about it—that his death would have to be, too. Isn't that what you said?"

I thought she might faint, she was so pale. "It's what I meant, Elsa. But I . . . I loved him so dearly."

"And you wouldn't have him leave you like this,"

said George, leaning back in his chair heavily, "penniless, when he'd promised you he'd be worth more dead than alive."

Clarice took a deep breath. "Well, all right," she snapped abruptly, the colour flooding to her cheeks. "If you don't want to help me, you can leave. I'm only sorry I made up your bed. If all you can do is make snide remarks . . ."

"Oh, but he's splendid," cut in Anthony. "We mustn't lose him. He looks facts right in the eye."

David had said nothing. He knew George better than I did; I had never been with them when they were actually on a case. I wondered at David's silence. But now he spoke confidently.

"George sometimes looks beyond the facts. What're you getting at, George?"

"Accident!" George snorted. "What flaming accident would make him disappear into fresh air? I don't think anybody's thought about it. This Konrad, he doesn't sound accident-prone to me. And if you won't accept suicide, which is the obvious thing, then there's something else as feasible as an accident, and we don't want to get involved with *that*."

"He's talking about murder," said David lightly, and the fork clattered from Amaryllis's hand to the floor. "Which is plain nonsense, of course, because of the cabinet against the door. Come on, George, admit it. Plain nonsense."

George lumbered to his feet. "Let's go and look at that blasted room," he said.

I had had a presentiment about this. He was not the George Coe I knew, vastly gentle and capable of ridiculous sentimentality. I assumed that David would be embarrassed for him, but no. He pushed back his chair, and he was quite calm, even smiling, when he took my arm.

"Do something, David," I whispered.

"Something?"

"To stop him. He's like a wild bull. He'll upset everybody."

"This is George, love. I can't change him." He grinned, challenging me. "And I couldn't manage without him. If he leaves, I do too."

"Sometimes I hate you, David."

"I know." He looked round before they all melted away. "Shall we all go up?" he asked.

There was silence. Amaryllis gave an exaggerated shudder. "Not for me."

"Especially you, my dear. You must have been there."

"Of course I was not!"

"You were his assistant. How could he experiment with his cabinet when his assistant wasn't there?"

She was rapidly losing interest in him, I was glad to see. Her poise was brittle. "Earlier. I was with him earlier. But I left him alone to play with his dummies."

David nodded, leading her on.

"Oh, you'll see," she told him angrily. "You don't need me. He used dummies in the cabinet when he fired into it. When there was no bullet in the dummy, then that was a success. You don't need me." She tossed her head. The slim neck was beginning to show the first wrinkles.

"But perhaps *he* did," David suggested, and something in her cracked. Her voice rose.

"He wanted me inside the damn thing!" she cried hysterically.

"Ah! Then you had no faith in it?"

"Go and check the dummies yourself!" she screamed. "Count the bullet holes, why don't you. See if you'd have stepped inside it!"

Then she turned away and walked rapidly down the ballroom, her head high but her movements so unco-ordinated that all the smooth flow of her limbs had become harsh.

I watched her walk away, and thought: but it was Konrad whose life was so heavily insured, when the danger was to her. Though he had been an escapologist earlier on, so no doubt the insurance cover was no more than theatrical advertisement after all.

"She walks," said David, "like some sort of mechanical doll."

I looked at him sharply, though of course he couldn't have known. But one of Amaryllis's stage characters as a ballet dancer had been the doll in *The Tales of Hoffmann*. I looked back at her. The hand reaching for the doorknob of the far door was moving with stiff blindness, a ballet movement.

Perhaps Amaryllis hadn't been quite so upset as she'd sounded.

"I'll show you the room," I said quietly.

THREE

In the end, only Auden Sundry and Anthony went with us to Konrad's laboratory-room.

We took oil-lamps; David, immediately behind me, carrying one, and Anthony with the other at the rear. The staircase up the Tower was not illuminated, although there was a complex of wiring in the workroom, for Konrad's bench.

The door into the Tower is beside the one to the battlements, opening from the Grand Gallery. The castle now seemed silent; it was its perpetual silence that had so haunted me the first few days I was there, the thick walls so effectively absorbing sound. The door closed behind us with a thud that sounded muffled.

I would have preferred not to lead. The stone staircase up the tower ran in a spiral round its perimeter, the walls pressing in at each shoulder, and because of the continuing curve the light danced in front of me, never quite reaching beyond the bend in front, and never illuminating more than four or five tapered steps ahead. Our voices reached beyond us and were lost.

I have never counted the steps. I had, always, to count the doors we passed, though I was told later that the latch on Konrad's door was different, more modern, than the rest, if you could call a huge wrought-iron ring modern. And his was the only one not rusted solid. At last I stopped.

"This is it."

I was reluctant to open that door. We stood, here, on one of the flat landings opposite each door, but these were only three feet wide. There was not much room, and the door was deeply set, heavy, oppressive. David reached past me.

"Let me."

He turned the ring and thrust the door open. It moved without sound. I felt quickly for the light switch inside, and the room was flooded with light.

It was naturally circular, some 30 feet across, the smooth curve of its walls broken only where the shape of the outer stairs intruded the inner wall of part of its spiral. Directly opposite the door was the only window, at that time closed. We moved inside. Anthony produced a slim cigarette-case and offered me one, smiling, as much as to say: "You see, I'm not such a cynical devil, really." But I was out of breath, and refused. Besides, I still thought he was.

The floor was bare boards, heavy, rough boards,

which echoed as we walked on them, there being so few floor coverings. This place was purely practical. In it, Konrad Klimax had created his illusions. Some of the old ones still stood around, not recognisable in their intention, but strangely pitiful and sordid away from their stage splendour. To one side, well clear of the door or window, was the workbench, and though tools and machinery have no specific meaning for me, it was clear that the equipment was comprehensive, and that Konrad had made all his equipment himself. Up above me the shadows ran high, the light not reaching because the pendant lamps were hung from open joists well clear of the actual ceiling.

David said: "It was . . . what time, Elsa?"

"After dinner. This time, perhaps."

"Then it'd be dark. Like now?"

"Yes."

"But you spoke of rushing up the stairs, and down again. In the dark?"

"We brought lamps, just like now. They're always to hand in case the power goes."

"Must have been unpleasant for you," he said, and I loved that tender undertone in his voice.

"Yes." I remembered my terror. "Yes." I looked away from Anthony, who was smiling. "The window wasn't closed."

David walked across and threw it open. It opened outwards, and the brisk wind at once caught it back against the outside wall. Lamps swung and swirled shadows up the wall, and the chill struck straight through my thin dress.

"Like this?" David called back.

"Yes. And just as cold."

"He wouldn't want to work with it open, then. So why did he open it?"

"To get out," suggested George. "To climb out."

But David had had to reach right out to retrieve the window catch. I caught my breath, although I had done so, too, on that night. The window, however, was sunk into an embrasure a foot deep, angling in to the actual opening, so that he could rest his stomach and chest on it for support. Easier for him than for me. He hesitated, looking upwards and down, before closing the window, and I knew what he would have seen by the light of the weak moon harassed by racing clouds.

He would have seen the bare, naked outer face of the Tower, plunging down to its origin on the cliff edge, and beyond that down again, the sea-slicked cliffs vertical for a further hundred feet, and finally the piled waves crashing into the cliff over peaks of rock, the water sucking and plunging round them.

The window slammed shut and David turned. The opening, though tall and narrow, would have allowed him to fall through.

"He could not possibly have lived," he decided.

George was prowling, hands in pockets, not touching anything. He did, though, pause at the small table to one side of the window, some ten feet into the room. He was looking down at the pistol which lay on it. Nothing else—just the pistol. He turned and asked me:

"Was this here then?"

"Yes."

"Just here? Exactly like this?"

"I . . . I think so. Though the police would've looked at it, and maybe moved it . . ."

"Police?" said David.

This, I knew, was one of his bland and innocent acts. I had mentioned the police to him earlier. He cocked an eyebrow at Anthony. "You sent for the police?"

"Who else could we send for—the fire brigade?"

David ignored the sarcasm. "You entered this room. The cabinet was hard against the door . . ."

"There it is, standing by the wall," put in Sundry.

"Yes. We'll consider that later. Perhaps Anthony will tell us exactly what happened."

"Surely your wife—"

"From you, if you don't mind."

Anthony shrugged. "You've already heard . . . there were the three of us, Clarice, Elsa and myself. The lights were on. The draught almost tore the door out of my hands, and your wife ran to look out of the window, then she struggled with it a bit and managed to shut it, and latched it. The women were . . . I suppose you'd call it shocked. I mean, it was staring us in the face. The room empty and the window open. But I had to make sure he'd . . . er . . . gone. The cabinet was the first idea, but he wasn't in there."

"Would there have been room for him?"

"Yes. I think the idea was to switch roles when he got it working, himself in the cabinet and Amaryllis with the gun. I don't know. But he made it big enough, so that's what I'd guess. It'd fallen on its back, so the door was on top, and I just lifted it. Empty, of course. Then I made a quick round of the room, looking at all the other equipment . . . some of the items he could well have hidden in . . ."

"That thought crossed your mind, did it, that he might have been hiding?"

"I don't know. Can't you see, I had to make sure! But, as you see, the room's so bare. There's the cupboards, but . . ." He strode across the room. You could hardly use the words 'back' and 'side' with a round room, but treating the door as the front and the window as the back, the row of cupboards was against the side wall to the right of the door, entering. Anthony flung open the doors. "You can see, nothing but his test dummies, they're all in here, except the one under the window."

David had had to lean over it to handle the window, as I had done on that night. It was the only one of the seven, in all, which was clothed. The rest hung in the cupboard in limp parade, sacking torsos, flabby arms and legs of calico stuffed with something, featureless faces hanging eyeless in dead gaze at the floor.

The one beneath the window was dressed in the female version of the illusionist's formal stage costume; tights, black pants, high-heeled shoes, a tricky set of tails, frilled shirt and white tie, and a shortened version of his shiny top hat, the whole thing incongruously crumpled and dishevelled in the corner of floor and wall beneath the window.

"It's the one he'd be using," explained Sundry, following our gaze.

"Then why is it dressed?" Dave asked.

Sundry touched the corner of his mouth. His nearly white hair shook untidily. "He'd want to create as near as possible the actual illusion."

"It would've been put in the cabinet, then, you think?"

"As far as he'd tell me anything, yes. He was to have given us a demonstration, but it was delayed. Things weren't going right. No, not right . . ." He looked mildly distressed.

"But why would it be there? It *was* there, Elsa?"

"It doesn't look as though it's been touched."

Anthony said: "I think I can explain that. As I said—when everybody assumed I was simply being ungracious—my father was driving himself insane with this. He was certainly verging on a breakdown. When it didn't work, which was nearly every time he tried it, he'd open the door of the cabinet, tear out the dummy, and he was big enough to do that with one hand, and throw it across the room in a fury."

"You mean you've seen him do that?"

"No. He wouldn't let me get near when he was testing. It was Amaryllis who told me that."

"So he'd let her watch, but nobody else?"

Anthony grinned. Sometimes his face could become quite attractive. "He'd have to let her watch, wouldn't he! The crazy madman actually expected her to go inside the damned thing."

"It is not a damned thing," said Sundry severely. "Whatever is certain, if Konrad made it, you can be sure it was ingenious and very dramatic."

"But you don't *know* that?" David asked.

A grumbling concern crept into Sundry's voice. "How can I know? We can't find his drawings and his description of operation. This is most annoying, as he's now dead, because he must have kept records, and we'd have expected him to file the details in our archives when it was perfected. But he's left nothing."

"So you've searched?"

"The whole castle, this room in detail, every habitable room. Of course we've searched."

"But I suppose you know what it was expected to do?"

"I know that much. I can even hazard a guess how." A gentle pride crept into his sonorous voice. "You want to know? Well . . ."

He turned his attention to the cabinet, with a decorous eagerness that betrayed him. He had been aching to put his hands on it. It now stood, on its castors, against the wall immediately behind the door as it opened, the wall that bore a frieze about three feet deep and 20 feet long, consisting entirely of glossy photos of Konrad Kilmax in performance, Amaryllis with him in most of them.

As I've said, the cabinet was about 18 inches square, and I now realised, not having seen it upright before, about seven feet all. It was of a deep rich and red wood, attractively carved on the corners, with a projecting architrave at top and bottom. As it was on castors, Sundry was able to sweep it out easily into the centre of the room. He opened the tall, narrow door.

Inside there was nothing but an empty cabinet. He put in his head, examining the inside, and only withdrew it when David asked:

"What is it supposed to do?"

Auden Sundry drew himself up. His fingers sneaked to his other cuff in a familiar gesture and his voice took on a different timbre—dramatic, intense. I could almost see him on the stage. (I *did* see him; I remembered suddenly his television series) I half expected him to begin: "Ladies and gentlemen . . ."

But he said: "He did tell me a little—quietly boasting, you know. You'll remember the cabinet that Anthony sneered at so patronisingly . . ." A twinkle there, a hint of reprimand. "Where the assistant climbed inside, the door was shut, and swords were then slid through it from all angles . . . you'll know that one?"

David nodded. George was standing by the end of the run of photographs, at his shoulder a number of panels leaning against the wall. George seemed bored, Anthony cynical. Sundry continued unabashed.

"Well, this is the modern version. The assistant would stand inside, and Konrad, or another assistant, would slam this door . . ." He slammed it, and I jumped. "Then Konrad, standing to one side, would at once—inside two seconds, he said—fire a bullet through the cabinet at chest height. From side to side, naturally, so as to preserve the door."

"A real bullet?"

"Oh, yes. See." And Sundry rotated the cabinet so that we could see the side panel. There was what looked like a bullet hole at about chest height.

"Looks like a .32," said David.

George roused. ".38."

He could hardly have seen from over there. I supposed that was the size of the gun on the table.

David said: "But he couldn't do that, not use a real gun on the stage. They wouldn't let him."

Sundry sighed. "I told him that. D'you think it'd stop him! He'd have hired a quarry or a firing range or something . . ."

"And made a right old performance out of it," said Anthony distastefully.

Sundry was amused. "But of course, my dear boy, he'd love the whole thing to be banned on the stage. The illusion they banned! You can see it on the posters. And he'd have the quarry or whatever floodlit, with an ambulance standing by . . ." Then he remembered what he had been saying, and shrugged. "But apparently it didn't work."

He rotated the cabinet. There was no hole in the other panel.

"Then the bullet didn't go through?"

Sundry nodded towards the dummy lying beneath the window. "You heard what Amaryllis said. A cupboard full of dummies with bullets in, and the thing thrown across the room. I could weep for him, that it failed."

We were silent, drawn into his personal mourning

for such a splendid illusion—which had failed.

"But not every time," said George, lumbering forward. He was carrying a dozen or so of the panels under his arm. "Spare side panels," he explained. "A trick like that . . . every time it worked he'd have a bullet hole through one panel and one out the other side. So he'd have to make 'em removable. These are his used ones. Have a look, Dave. Some with clean entry holes—you can see they're .38s—and some with ragged exit holes. Count 'em. I have. Every time you get a pair that match, that's a successful try. Single entries with no exits matching, that's a failure. I make it eight successes, seven failures. Not so bad as all that. Oh, no."

"And he didn't live to demonstrate it," said Sundry sadly.

"Eight of each," said David, "with this last failure."

Evens. That wasn't bad enough to justify suicide. I began to warm to George. He was beaming.

"So . . ." went on David, "this other failure . . . he threw the doll across the room and under the window, which was open. Why the hell'd it be open, George?"

"Perhaps he got all worked up, and warm."

David turned to me. "Elsa?" His voice was sharp; suddenly he was not my David.

"It was dreadfully cold," I said, and heard how flat was my own voice.

David grinned without humour. "A window open, for no purpose, and perhaps the eight successes were the first, and the eight failures the last."

"Oh, come on, Dave," George growled amiably. "He didn't commit suicide. An accident perhaps. The cabinet, standing maybe where it is now . . ." He ambled over to it, rested one huge hand against the top architrave, and tilted it towards the door. "And it fell, or was pushed. An accident. Perhaps he stumbled—"

"Rubbish," cut in Anthony with contempt. "The man's manic, I do believe. Shouting his head off downstairs, trying to prove one thing, and now babbling away about the opposite. Of course it didn't fall over, you great idiot. If it had, the top of it would have been against the door. But it wasn't. The castors on the bottom were pushing against the door. You don't have to take my word for it. Ask her." And he pointed a finger at me, almost in accusation.

Poor George. So pleased with himself, and I had to say: "He's quite correct, George. The castors *were* against the door."

I turned to David for some sort of guidance, not knowing what to expect from George, and to my surprise David was watching his friend with a slight smile, I thought of challenge. When I looked back at him, George stuck out his lower lip, hunched his shoulders, and wandered away with his hands in his pockets.

And that was about all there was, except for the long, tiring period when George and David searched the place, I don't know what for. Anthony and Auden Sundry left, and very soon I was wishing I had, too, though I could not now face that staircase alone.

The dummies in the cupboard proved to be full of bullets, or at least, if not full, proved to show evidence of bullets. Their upper bodies were full of sand, which, David told me, was the reason the shots had not completely gone through them. The gun, George declared, he being something of an expert, was a .38 automatic pistol, and could have fired them. All very technical, but it didn't seem to get anywhere.

They even experimented with the cabinet, though they could find no way, even with it standing right against the door before it was toppled, that in falling it would come to rest, on its back, with its castors against the door. They were always eighteen inches away.

I became very bored with it, and not at all certain what they were trying to prove.

When eventually we did get back to our rooms, I asked David: "I don't see what you're trying to prove."

"Nothing, my sweet. Just a preliminary look round."

"Then why were you so pleased when George started coming out with theories?"

He was loosening his tie, tossing it over a chair back. "You have to get him involved. He's a cynical devil—won't believe anything but the worst about people's motives. It was a relief to see him getting his brain working. And now . . . you just try stopping him."

It was late. I like a hot drink before bed, and said I'd go down to the kitchen. "Tea," said David, who lives on it, so I paused only to knock on George's door to see if he wanted any, but there was no response.

"George isn't in his room," I said, when I got back with the tray. I felt vaguely worried.

"You can bet he wouldn't be. I'll tell you where he is. He's up in that Tower, and he'll be there for hours. I know him."

"And if I wasn't here, underfoot, you'd be there too?"

"But you are, love, and the Tower's got no appeal."

So the nightdress I put on was only a vague, shimmering mystery, and after all I hadn't seen him for a fortnight, and I was combing my hair out, watching David in the mirror—pacing the floor in his pyjamas and not yet relaxed—when George burst into the room with barely a knock.

"Dave, the gun jammed."

He had it in his hand. He turned and waved it at me.

David sighed. "George, we love to see you. But, as you'll notice, we were about to go to bed."

"Yes, yes, I see," he agreed, peering at me. "Sorry, Elsa. But Dave . . ."

I got up and reached for the matching négligé, which, I'm afraid, barely improved the obscurity. "Go on, George, say it."

"It's just . . . just . . ." He recovered. "He tried to fire a second shot. Look, the gun jammed with the trigger back. See, Elsa, here . . ."

He came across and bent over me.

"I do see, George. I'll take your word for it. Somebody tried to fire a second shot."

George was triumphant. "Now . . . how does *that* fit in? This Konrad, we've heard about him firing a shot into his cabinet. But there wasn't any mention of him firing two, or even trying to. It wouldn't fit the illusion, anyway. Does it mean it wasn't him who fired the gun this last time? Does it, Dave?"

I looked at my lustful and loving husband. His eyes were bright, his hand reaching for the gun. I sighed.

"George, would you like a cup of tea? It'll still be hot."

"Thank you, Elsa," he said absently. I might not have been there.

FOUR

In the end we got very little sleep. But when we went down for breakfast George wasn't there, and Sundry said he'd eaten earlier and disappeared. And we know where, do we not!

David was now keen to get on with things. Before the appearance of George with the jammed gun I'd felt that David's interest was mainly a deference to my own support of Clarice, but now he was all eagerness. Some thought had captured his attention, and I rather hoped that it was not the attempt to fire a second shot. After all—and had he thought of this?—that gun had lain there on the table for several days, and anyone could have picked it up, and attempted to fire it, if only from curiosity. The police, perhaps. They had been to the castle and made their observations, but there had been no suggestion of foul play, so that the gun had been of no specific interest to them. But, nevertheless, they might have handled it, and I hoped that David was not building a theory based on anything so flexible.

But I might have trusted him more. When I returned from my walk he was on the phone in the library to a police sergeant, who, apparently, was swearing that none of his squad had picked up the pistol.

I had gone out because those massive walls were beginning to press in on me, and because David wanted to talk to Clarice and I didn't wish to embarrass him by being there. It was not a morning for walking, although the wind had eased and I welcomed its freshness, but clouds were massing on the horizon and were being torn free in streamers, and showers spattered at me from time to time.

The tide was slack. We had been told that the currents in these parts would most likely take a body well out to sea, and that there was only a slight chance of it washing ashore again, and even then possibly miles along the coast. But, walking along the cliff-top, I could not keep my eyes from the sullen water, and found myself examining every exposed area of sand. There was nothing, of course, and I walked barely a mile before turning back. I had wanted to reach the lighthouse, but it was farther away than I had expected.

There was no sign of any other habitation in the whole extended sweep of the countryside. A few sheep grazed, and once I thought I heard a tractor. But I could not see it. Always, there was the persistent crash of the sea; and once, the thud of hooves.

I stood still, trying to locate the sound. Between me and the castle there was a small copse, which seemed to hang right to the edge of the cliff, so that I was about to turn inland to skirt it when suddenly a bay burst into sight from around the trees, its rider flat along its neck. And screaming. There was the sudden flash of her face as she turned to glance back, the wind caught her hair, and again she screamed—that mock fear of a woman pursued—and on a grey, in superb control, Anthony appeared after her.

Then she saw me, and swerved in my direction. This was strange, if her fear had been assumed. It seemed for one terrible moment that she would ride me clear over the cliff, then she caught the horse into a plunging swerve, and in the second before it settled, snorting, I saw a strange look in her eyes, something very close to terror.

Anthony eased his pace well short of us, and cantered up. I wondered whether he had deliberately given himself time to control his expression. If so, he'd not succeeded. There was a tight jut to his jaw that even affected his voice.

"Not weather for a walk, Elsa."

"Bracing," I said, ridiculously defensive. "I was just on my way back."

Amaryllis slid down from the saddle lightly. "Do you mind if I join you? I think I'll walk home, too."

And it was Anthony who replied for me. "Please yourself."

She looked up at him. "You don't need me, Anthony." And he pulled the grey's head around viciously, riding away at full gallop.

We walked in silence for a minute or two. The bay mare nuzzled my neck. At last:

"A dangerous place to ride so fast," I said.

Her eyes were laughing. "Life'd be very dull without danger and excitement. Don't you feel that?"

"I don't find it dull. But I did wonder . . . and now you've explained it."

"I didn't explain anything."

"Why you exchanged ballet for the rather . . . brash, shall we say . . . the brash but exciting world of the vaudeville stage."

"But ballet was wildly exciting, my dear."

"So I was wrong," I admitted.

"A different excitement, that was all." She turned her head and smiled at me. "You see, there was Konrad. And also . . ." She laughed, but there were tears in it. ". . . also, I discovered I would never reach the top in ballet."

"But how could you be so sure?"

"Oh, my *entrechats* were perfect, and my *pirouettes en arabesque* were a dream. But I couldn't project. I was only a dancer and not an interpreter."

I glanced at her. She had been speaking in angry rejection. I couldn't help being a little disparaging. "I've heard that sort of thing before."

"But I *knew*. I got support parts—a cygnet in *Swan Lake*, the cossack girl in *La Boutique Fantasque*. And of course I loved the music. And then—I was in an offshoot company of the Royal Ballet and we were playing the Grand at Wolverhampton—Dasha Baryshkova was taken ill, and I got to dance the part of Olympia, the mechanical doll, in *The Tales of Hoffmann*. Oh, that suited me fine, suited my style, because then—now, to some extent—I was supple and skinny . . . I thought I'd make a splendid doll. You know the story, coming alive when Hoffmann puts on the magic glasses, then collapsing as a doll again when he takes them off. I danced my heart out . . . and it flopped."

"Oh, my dear . . ."

"Don't be sorry, it was the night of my life. Konrad had been in the wings—his show was due on the following week—and he came to the dressing-room to see me. And even . . . even informal, he was completely overpowering. And being Konrad, quite honest of course. He said . . ." She attempted his deep, fluent voice, but grotesquely. "'A fair performance, young lady, but you're wasting your talents.' So I simply stayed behind when the company moved on, and the following week I was sawn in half. And then, we began to develop his famous Coppélia illusion."

"Coppélia? But . . ."

She stopped, releasing the horse, who at once began to crop the meagre grass. "You haven't *seen* it?"

I shook my head.

She sat down on an outcrop of rock. "Then I must tell you. It was superb!" I sat beside her. She was animated and alive, her hands fluid, all her body lithe and moving to the memory. "We called it Coppélia, because people know the name, though of course the doll never dances in Coppélia, it's simply Coppélia pretending to be a doll, and anyway Konrad preferred the music of Delibes. But to that music we did the Olympia *pas de deux* from *Hoffmann*."

"That'd be sacrilege, surely."

"Entertainment. We did it in style, with a recording from Coppélia, Konrad in old-fashioned evening dress as Hoffmann, and some extra from the show as Spalanzani, to hand him the magic spectacles. The curtain would go up on me, centre stage, sitting as a floppy doll in a plain chair, then Konrad'd see me, fall in love with me on sight . . . dear Konrad . . . he'd take the glasses, and I'd come alive. And I'd dance—God, how I'd dance!—and Konrad would do a few steps with me. Then I'd dance to a climax, all *grand jetés* and *tours en l'air*, Konrad'd tear off his spectacles and hold out his arms and begin to walk towards me—and I'd collapse in a crumpled heap when the magic disappeared. Then there'd be a drum roll, he'd slowly walk towards me, bend over me and pick me up in his arms, and I'd be all limp and lifeless. And suddenly . . . in the ballet he'd have simply walked off, dragging the doll behind him . . . but suddenly he'd go into a rage that I was only a doll, and he'd tear me apart, limbs tossed everywhere, sawdust flying, and the head . . . he'd clutch it to his chest, weeping, as the spot faded and the curtain came down."

She stopped. I might not have been there. Her eyes were on the grey horizon.

"Very impressive," I murmured.

"Impressive! It was drama, it was superb, it was class! We brought the house down."

"And it came to an end?"

She spread her hands, the fingers spatulate. "You can't live for ever on the same illusion, and it all hung on one slim thread of deception. Konrad had to think again and find more drama, more impact . . ."

She was on her feet, clicking her tongue for the mare. I said: "So he came up with the cabinet?"

"And he expected me to go inside the bloody thing!" she cried.

"When it was safe."

"Safe! It was never going to be safe."

"But surely it was improving."

"Ha!" It was a harsh little exclamation of contempt. "The first seven or eight tries, with the dummies—oh, it worked. But the last few times . . . Elsa, I stood there, four times, at his elbow, when he fired the gun, and I'll swear I heard the thud of that bullet going into the dummy. And that could've been me!"

We were walking, now more quickly, agitation springing her step. "Four?" I asked. "There were eight failures."

"I refused to stay and watch." She flashed an angry look at me. "It turned my stomach."

"I imagine it would. But you were there that night?"

"Sometimes we simply tested the cabinet—no gun—both of us properly dressed for the part. That I'd do. But he loaded his gun . . . so I went. Oh, I'm not telling a lie, I was out of there like a shot. And d'you know, when I got back to my room I was shaking, and absolutely sticky with perspiration. I took a bath, and changed—started to—and then I heard the fuss along the Gallery . . ."

I knew then why she was telling me all this. She was explaining that Konrad's career had been failing, his new illusion refused to work, and his assistant was losing her nerve—more, she was deserting him—more even, she was in love with Konrad's son, and she'd been Konrad's mistress. She was telling me we were wasting our time, and that he'd clearly had reasons for committing suicide.

I wondered whom she was protecting.

But nevertheless I told it all in detail to David. I found him in the Cleric's Library, making that phone-call to the police sergeant that I mentioned. He had been using the Library as an interview-room, and had just finished a long conversation with Clarice.

He listened attentively to my story, nodding, smoking steadily. "There's a possibility that she even arranged the excuse to walk back with you," he said at the end.

"No. I'm sure her fear was real."

"But you say she's in love with Anthony?"

How can you explain to a man? "Yes."

He shrugged. "But did she tell you how the cabinet worked?"

"No. I tried to get it out of her, but she said it was a secret—Konrad's secret. David, they're all completely absorbed in this mystery business. You'd think it was sacred."

"To them it is."

"But do you think she's correct—about Konrad?" I asked.

He considered that. "The atmosphere and the background for suicide were there. But he was quite an expert at creating atmosphere, and from what Clarice says . . . what're you smiling at?"

"David, she's a determined woman. It's what she wants—your help to save her insurance money. And she's got right into your gullible mind. No, I'm not being cynical. I remember . . . she wanted to be captain of the hockey team. She couldn't play the game, but nevertheless she wanted to be captain, and by heaven she was."

"I thought she was your friend."

I laughed. "She is. I love her. But *you* don't need to, David."

"I don't know what *anybody* wants any more," he complained, rubbing his hand through his hair.

I laughed at his confusion. "Shall I tell you what I want?"

"And we'll work to that? Right."

"Just the truth of it all."

The trouble was that I was beginning to understand his ridiculous, and until now irritating, drive for the truth, as though it was the most wonderful thing in the world. It was convenient in some ways; when he made a promise it was given in truth, and kept inflexibly. Mind you, it made him a little chary of promises. But not this time.

"That you shall have, my sweet."

Then at once, ridiculously, I began to feel nervous of what I had provoked. I steered away from it. "And what was it Clarice told you?"

"Oh . . . that. Well, that Konrad could not, ever, leave anything looking like it really was."

"That's a great help."

"But she was sincere."

"Yes."

"And now, there's just Anthony to see."

"He's out riding."

"Then perhaps you can confirm what Clarice told me, that after you ran downstairs . . ."

"Confirm it! But you said she was sincere."

"The best liars always are."

After I'd finished laughing, and he watching me ruefully because he had been serious, I said:

"What did she tell you?"

"Only that she'd been very brave . . . she's a splendid woman, Elsa . . ."

"What did she *say*?"

He grinned. "Her own words, that she'd been brave in the room, kind of stunned with shock, until you ran out to get to a phone, then she went all to pieces. So Anthony took her down after you, and to her room, and at that time she saw you along the Gallery . . ."

"Yes. I'd tried the phone in our room, but it wasn't working. They go off and on with no excuse at all, so I'd come out on the Gallery, intending to try the one in the room that George is in now. I saw Clarice, with

Anthony, just leaving the Tower door, and him with his arm around her as though she needed the support. Then the phone in George's room worked and I made the call, and I went out again, and Amaryllis called to me from her room door along the other end of the Gallery, asking what had happened. She was in pants and bra in her doorway, and by that time Anthony was halfway down the staircase, with Auden Sundry walking up to meet him, and him asking what was all the fuss. And then Martin Fisher came in through the back of the hall, which meant he'd been out in the courtyard, and we were all together in the Pink Lounge when that very nice police sergeant arrived."

"Elsa," he said, "we're very lucky to have had you on the spot. An uninvolved witness who actually sees things! You can't imagine how rare that is." He glanced at his watch. "I wonder when Anthony will be back."

"Then you don't believe me!"

"Of course I do. All I want to ask him is why he hated his father."

"But, David, that must be obvious. Anthony's a conjuror. He does it all with his hands and his technique. Konrad had the deepest contempt for him. Conjuring, he said, was just a paltry thing compared with the art of illusion, which requires showmanship and personality. And, of course, Anthony hates illusions. He says they depend on the equipment and not the man."

"You gathered all this in less than a week?"

"I've never known anything about this sort of thing, so of course it all had to be explained to me. They used to compete for my attention, and my sympathy I suppose."

"Yes, I can understand that." He looked at me

solemnly. "And who won?"

"Nobody won, David. Don't be ridiculous. But Konrad was inflexibly charming, and Anthony has always . . . well, frightened me, I suppose."

"Then I *must* have a talk with him. *I've* never managed to frighten you, so there's obviously a secret to be learned."

"You dare!"

He grinned. "Let's see who else we can find."

The music drew us to the Pink Lounge. It is the most relaxing room in the castle, possibly because the wall hangings of heavy Persian rugs—which in fact were introduced by Anthony for his hi-fi; something to do with resonance or eigentones, I think—did at least serve to hide the bleak stone walls. The furniture, too, was less repressive there, chosen specifically for comfort and intended to be moved around to obtain the best position for television or stereo, or even the old-fashioned pleasure of simply reading a book.

Anthony was playing Delibes, the ballet music from Coppélia, second act. He was lying on his shoulders in a huge easy chair, indolent, and insolent with his brusque gesture for silence when David attempted to speak to him.

David shrugged. Casually he wandered the room. I found a seat, as far away from Anthony as possible. I could feel he was waiting for something.

It came just before the ending of the act. Amaryllis entered, with Martin at her shoulder. The music caught her, froze her. Anthony looked round, smiling, then he reached forward and switched it off.

That was all we had of that little scene. Ten seconds, perhaps. But Amaryllis was plainly shaken, and I thought she would turn and leave. Something had been said, and I had not understood what. Then her head came up and she calmly walked forward and examined the record sleeves he had taken out.

"But I thought you were a Stravinsky addict, Anthony," she said blithely. "You don't have to play my music just to please me, you know."

The emotion of the moment had gone. I didn't think David had noticed it, and I was not even sure it had not been imagination. But if it was not . . . I could see what Anthony was doing, and with a certain sort of woman the technique probably worked, those with a masochistic streak. They'd welcome the rejection and the insults, the implied danger. And, come to think of it, there was a facet of masochism in being an illusionist's assistant; there might not have been actual physical danger involved, but the possibility lurked behind the deception. I watched his dark eyes on her. He was playing with a deck of cards, fanning them, disappearing them, and when she bent close to him, studiously ignoring his activities as she reached for a cigarette from the box, he plunged his fingers for her corsage and produced a card from it. He displayed it to her, and she recoiled. It was the ace of spades.

David was saying: "If we could have a few words, Mr Fisher . . . In the Library, I'd suggest."

Martin and David headed for the door. I didn't want to remain with the stifling atmosphere, though Clarice walked in at that moment and blissfully ignored it, chattering away about where was her recording of *The Student Prince*. I followed them into the Library.

David wanted to hear the details of the insurance policy. Martin Fisher, I already knew, had come to the castle as a guest, but really as an observer for his company, to see and assess the new illusion. The cover was on Konrad's life, and for some years now, since he gave up escapology, Konrad had been in no danger at all from his equipment. But formalities had to be observed. In the old days the insurance company had had to know the secrets of his famous escapes from tanks full of water while handcuffed and chained, to satisfy themselves that their vaunted double-indemnity clause was not sheer folly on their part. And so Fisher had been at the castle, as had Auden Sundry on behalf of his Magic Circle, to see the new illusion working. It was strange that the financial aspect would reveal the cabinet's secrets to Fisher, while Sundry would have had to wait for Konrad's death.

"This double-indemnity . . ." said David.

"His life's insured for £100,000," said Fisher. "Ordinary life cover, with the usual provisions. The premiums were huge, of course. Which . . ." He bounced eagerly, bright eyes darting from one to the other of us. ". . . which, I don't mind telling you, he was finding it more and more difficult to pay."

"He doesn't have to pay them any more."

"No. Though there's no proof of death yet."

"So you'd hold back payment?"

"Of course. Of course, dear sir. We haven't had an inquest yet, anyway. There can't even be a claim without some legal evidence of death. And as . . . as things stand—and I'm sure you're well aware of this—the verdict is surely going to be suicide."

David nodded. "Which would suit you, I've no doubt. Because then your company would pay nothing."

"It'd suit the company, not me. The Kleins have become personal friends over the years. Theirs has always been my own account. I am particularly fond of Clarice."

David leaned back, relaxing. This was just a friendly chat. "Yes, I can see. It makes it a bit awkward for you, doesn't it! For your company, you've got to push for a suicide verdict, or at least hope for one. You'd hate yourself for it." And David smiled.

Fisher almost laughed at him. "You're overdramatising it, my friend. There comes a point where professional considerations override personal issues. My basic loyalty has to be to my company."

"And to the percentage commission you'd get for saving your company £100,000. If, of course, you were in a position to influence the outcome."

I hadn't known that David could be so casually insulting. I was not sure I liked it. But he didn't meet my eye, and I carefully remained silent.

And Fisher, too, surprised me. Suddenly his voice was sharp, and his bounce became stilled. "There'd be no commission. There's been no claim."

"But if there is . . ." David's voice was gentle.

"Then I'll fight it. Damn it all—you do your job and I'll do mine."

"I am doing mine. With the knowledge I have at the moment I don't think he took his own life." So casual. Dear David.

Fisher actually managed a sneer. "That's *your* fee talking."

"Now there I'm at an advantage, because there isn't one. It leaves things open. Clarice is simply a friend." He grinned. "Not as long-standing a friendship as yours, I must admit."

"Then I think I hope you'll succeed," said Fisher, and at once he was his old self, his eyes alight with mockery. "With whatever it is you're trying to do. I hope you know."

David relaxed. He laughed. "At this stage, I'm not quite sure."

Martin Fisher left us. His brief snap of anger had

been provoked only by the slight to his integrity. Having established it he was alive and full of energy again. The door closed behind him.

"I don't think he can even trust himself," said David. Then he turned and smiled at me. "Why is Anthony doing that to Amaryllis?" he asked.

I looked at him in surprise. "You realised? But I told you, David. He loves her."

He grimaced. "I'll have to take your word for it, though it's a funny way to go about things. But I didn't quite mean that. Put it another way. Why was the music expected to upset her?"

"Because she failed at ballet, or at least believes she did."

"Or because *that* music was used for the doll illusion on the stage?"

"It could be that."

"But she loved working that illusion . . . the way she spoke to you about it. How, then, could its music upset her?"

"It's finished, David. It's been finished for some time, and she loved it because it combined working with Konrad with her beloved ballet. But now . . . now there was going to be nothing more glamorous than being fired at in a wooden cabinet. Perhaps Anthony is taunting her with that."

"Telling her," he mused, "that now she's got nothing."

We looked at each other. I couldn't help shuddering. There was something in David's eyes I had not seen before.

Then the door bounced open and George came in, excited and red in the face.

"Dave, you ever read any Edgar Allan Poe?"

We stared at him.

FIVE

For this, it seemed, we had need of Auden Sundry. We found him walking the battlements in a huge old greatcoat and declaiming from *Hamlet*.

"I wanted to be an actor," he said, the mood still gripping him so that he bent gravely over my hand and kissed it. "We must now all take arms against a sea of troubles."

"We need you in the room to do a bit of opposing," said David. "You'll want to take charge of his drawings and descriptions."

"His . . . You *found* them? Good Lord! But we covered every inch!"

"George found them."

We trooped up the spiral staircase, George in the lead like a huge, excited schoolboy. He flung open the door.

From his manner I had expected papers to be strewn over the table, but it was bare. George had the lights on because, although it was not yet noon, the window was too small to admit much light. Everything seemed as it had been.

"I remembered Poe," George explained. "I read him when I was a kid. 'The Purloined Letter'. Remember? The room was searched and searched for that document, because they assumed it'd be well hidden away. And all the time, there it was where a letter's supposed to be—in the letter-rack. So I thought, where else to hide his plans and descriptions than in plain sight?"

He began to unpin the black-and-white photographs from the board along the wall. They were all ten by eights, from way back when Konrad hung face down in glass-fronted tanks, to more recent days when Amaryllis graced the stage with him. George put them in a pile on the table, and simply turned them over. There, on their backs, were the details of every illusion Konrad Klimax had used, progressing gradually to the cabinet.

Beside me, Sundry took a deep, sighing breath, and reached out his hands, his fingertips lightly brushing them. "This makes me happier than I ever expected to be in this benighted castle."

Then he turned away, as though the emotion stifled him.

I was surprised that he hadn't pounced on them. "But the drawings are there," I said. "There'll be details of how the cabinet worked. Don't you want to see?"

"I know how it worked."

"But you always said—"

"Out of loyalty to a dear friend, Elsa. But I'm not inexperienced. Naturally I saw how it would work, and what he intended. Or at least, how it *had* to work."

"You sound sad."

He smiled into eternity above my shoulder. "Because it could never have been used, that's why. Oh, I made some remark about him using an empty quarry or a firing range, but that was my enthusiasm breaking free. In practice, it would have needed a stage, careful curtaining, special lighting—and he would not have been allowed to use the gun."

George spoke roughly, I thought, breaking the mood. "Then come and explain it to us."

"If I must. But what good can it do you now?"

"I don't know," said David. "But tell us."

"Then I don't need his drawings."

And George, completely deflated, watched him morosely as he went over to the cabinet. The drawings he had spent so many hours to discover were, it seemed, purely of academic interest.

"You could have said," he grumbled.

Sundry turned, with one of his charming smiles. He wheeled the cabinet into the centre of the room. I was vaguely aware that Fisher had entered the room. Without looking at him I could feel his anxious interest.

Sundry flung open the cabinet's door. "You see, empty," he declaimed in a stage voice. He slapped the inside surfaces to prove it. "But you'll notice that the corner uprights are rather more solid than the sides, if only to hold the whole thing rigid. In practice, they'll be hollow, with inside each one a tiny compressed-air bottle. And what Konrad has done—this being his genius—is arrange a series of arms and levers so that a touch on a switch or a valve sends the base, on which the assistant would be standing, lifting up rapidly to the top."

He ran his fingers up and down the edges of the door opening. "Ah, I see. There's a valve operated by the door itself. Shut the door, and the lifting floor operates automatically. It probably took a second, maybe two. Konrad spoke of two seconds before he fired a shot through the cabinet."

At the thought I felt a prickling down my spine. No wonder Amaryllis had been determined not to be his assistant on this one.

"And what position is it in now?" David asked.

"I'd say . . . yes . . . in the operated position. The platform's at the top. A pity. We might have tried it, but I just can't see . . ."

George was standing at the table, riffling through the photos. "It's all here," he said in a bored voice. "If anybody'd care to look. There's a lever, just at the bottom, behind—"

"I have it," Sundry cut in, his voice mildly excited, and he stood back as the platform slid downwards with a gentle hiss. "I wonder . . . if he didn't need fresh air bottles for each attempt . . . perhaps we might try it with a dummy."

"I see no reason why not," said David solemnly.

Sundry was delighted. His step was eager as he moved towards the dummy beneath the window.

"No, not that one," said David sharply. "One out of the cupboard."

Sundry raised his eyebrows in surprise, but nevertheless went to get one.

Theoretically the dummies would have to weigh the same as the proposed victim, Amaryllis. I doubted she was much above six stone, say 90 pounds. Sundry returned with the dummy clasped to him, making the effort one would expect for such a weight. It was limp, but once he'd got it inside, the cabinet itself held it upright. Sundry poised the door.

"Ready?"

We were certainly ready. David nodded, and Sundry slammed the door. Then, magnificently, soundlessly, the dummy popped out of the top, though, being limp, it at once flopped over and fell down to the floor at our feet.

"Working all right now," said David, his voice expressionless.

I was feeling breathless, just from watching it. The whole operation had taken no more than a second, and in fact the dummy had made a small leap into the air at the top.

"It would of course take some considerable experience on the assistant's part," said Sundry with some doubt. "Most people would simply black-out. She'd need training, rather like the astronauts. You can see how far ahead Konrad's thinking was. All the modern sciences."

"But . . ." David was frowning. "It'd need some sort of cover. As it is now, she'd simply appear in plain sight of the audience."

"It's all here," George cut in, "if you'd only take the time to read it. There's a curtain or something comes down at the front, just level with the top edge. Damn it all, it'd be bloody obvious."

"No." Sundry was gentle. "The lighting would see to that. This is why I said it would need a stage. All that sort of thing is part of the illusionist's expertise. It's all a matter of lighting and the deflection of interest. Konrad to one side, with the gun levelled. All eyes would be on the centre of the cabinet, and not the top. In practice, she'd reach up for a trapeze, or something like that, behind the forward curtain. There'd be the terrific emotional impact of the shot, the wood actually splintering from the cabinet walls, and he'd fling open the door, and she'd be gone. He could then tilt the cabinet, remove the top platform if he liked, and show it empty from top to bottom, restore it, shut the door, and she could be back there, inside, in five seconds."

If, I thought grimly, she was still alive. And nobody seemed pleased. George I could understand; he was like a child, eager in his discovery of a profound fact of life, only to be told: yes, dear, now go and play. David I could not understand. He was tense, his eyes deep and . . . hurt? Yes, hurt. Sundry was clearly disappointed, in spite of his professional enthusiasm, that Konrad had not explored more deeply into the untried. And Fisher? I looked at him, and realised that he was, of all of us, quite delighted.

"Well," he claimed, "that explains how the cabinet got itself against the door." He looked round for approval. "Well, doesn't it? You saw—that thing's quite powerful. It's like a gun, shooting the dummy out. And every action has an equal and opposite reaction. I learnt that at school. The dummy shot up because the cabinet pressed down against the floor."

Dear man, he was quite excited. David smiled at him. "So?"

"So imagine that Konrad had got it standing with its door facing the room door, with the dummy inside. You saw how Auden slammed it . . . well, perhaps Konrad slammed the cabinet door a little too hard, and the cabinet toppled over backwards as it operated. Then the dummy would be thrown out sideways instead of upwards—landing where it is now, under the window—and the cabinet itself, which would be perched on a couple of its castors at that time, would shoot back against the door."

"And?" asked David calmly.

"He threw himself out of the window."

The abrupt, slightly ridiculous, ending to his explanation annoyed me. And the reasoning was so self-contradictory that I could not help bursting in: "But surely . . ."

Then David turned to me, eyes grave, his mouth stern. And he smiled. "You tell him, Elsa." As though it might come better from a woman!

"Well, it seemed to me . . . if the dummy was thrown out, that was what it was supposed to do, and that would surely mean a success for Konrad. Poor man, and Amaryllis has told me how his first few attempts were successful, and only the later ones failures. So it does seem rather strange that he'd take his life if he'd just achieved a success." I looked at Fisher sadly. He had a tendency to splutter when he was building up to an angry outburst. "Really, you know," I said, trying to be kind, "you should think more about it before pouncing in, though we can all appreciate how very much you'd prefer it to be suicide."

"Damn it all, it explains—"

"No, no. It doesn't. Because, you see, it wasn't a successful attempt, because there's only one bullet hole in the cabinet wall. Where did that bullet go except into the dummy? So it couldn't have shot out. And anyway, when you come to think of it, if the cabinet toppled, as you suggested, Martin, would Konrad even fire his shot, and if he did, he'd surely have had difficulty even hitting the cabinet while it was toppling. So really, you know, the whole idea isn't very sound. Do you think I said that right, David?"

"I couldn't have put it better," he said, and his eyes were smiling.

"Women's logic!" cried Fisher, more savagely than I thought the situation deserved. "But Clarice is your friend, of course."

"But you said she's yours, too," I said, annoyed myself.

David spoke with that quiet voice that means he's close to the danger point. I glanced at him warningly, but he said it, just the same.

"Fisher's naturally worried about losing £200,000. Don't worry, Elsa, he's not as stupid as he sounded. He can see what it means."

"What the hell d'you mean, £200,000!" Martin shouted. "That's the double-indemnity . . ."

"Ah!" David sounded disappointed. "I was wrong, Elsa, he *is* as stupid as—"

"What're you trying to do to me!"

And behind us George laughed. I was sorry for Martin, but he'd brought it on himself. He seemed trapped, and not sure by what. He looked round wildly, and Sundry tapped him on the shoulder.

"Better listen to what he's got to say."

"Yes," said David, "if you'll stop jumping about for a bit. Actually, your idea about the cabinet sliding back was quite good. Valid, I think. It'd explain how it got like that, and in a logical way. I wasn't too keen with the idea that he'd simply shoved it there, just to make sure that nobody thought there was anybody else in here with him. Yes, I do think the cabinet toppled as it operated, and shot back, like a cannon firing, against the door."

"Will you say it!" said Fisher tensely.

"You want to tell him, George?"

"No." And George, too, sounded violent.

"Ah, well . . ." David shrugged. "Look at it like this. Assume, as we've got to, that he was trying his cabinet, and it was standing just like Martin said it was, with its door facing the room door. And once again it failed. When he fired his shot his dummy hadn't moved. So . . . as Anthony explained . . . he'd open the cabinet door and yank the dummy out and toss it to where it is now, under the window. And then what'd he do? Well, we've seen our friend Auden sticking his head inside . . . I'd suggest that Konrad did much the same. His first thought'd be to find out what had gone wrong. And maybe he stumbled, had to step forward to save himself, and found himself actually inside the thing. Then, with his stumbling and what-not, it'd perhaps topple over backwards, just as Martin said it could have done. Only maybe it was closer to the window than we've got it now, and, as it fell over, the door fell shut. And then . . . ironical when you come to consider it . . . then he achieved his first success for quite a while, and it projected him out in an arc, through the window, and at the same time the cabinet shot back against the door, as it was found. Doubly ironical, really, because Martin's helped us to see the truth, which is that Konrad died during the operation of an illusion, and cost Martin's company £200,000."

"I'm not having it!" shouted Fisher frantically, but Sundry walked forward and solemnly shook David's hand, no doubt eternally grateful for David's help for his life-long friend's widow. Then why did I imagine that his quiet smile was just a little cynical?

"Better go and tell the widow, hadn't we?" asked George.

I didn't know what to make of George. It was not like him to sulk, but he was giving the appearance of still resenting the lack of appreciation for his own bit of detection.

"Better bring your photos along, George," I said, seeing that David was heading for the door. "I think it was a simply splendid piece of reasoning, finding those drawings."

He looked down at my arm, and his heavy face lightened for a moment. Then he shook his head stubbornly. "No, it wasn't. Poe thought of it first. But, Elsa, have you thought, if Auden Sundry knew how it operated, why didn't he say so? And I'll bet he knew where the drawings were, all the time."

"Now, George, you mustn't be angry with him. I'm sure he'd have said, in due course."

"When it seemed we weren't going to come across them, you mean?"

"I *didn't* mean that. You're acting very strangely, George."

"I'm simply wondering how many more things he would have brought to our attention, if we hadn't got round to them." He shook his head shaggily, worried. "Come on, Elsa, we're going to lose them if we don't hurry."

"Leave it to David to break the news." I was feeling relieved that it was over, and refused to be concerned about George's premonitions. Now I couldn't wait to get away from the place. I hadn't realised how much the sombre atmosphere of the castle was depressing me.

"Pleased?" he asked.

"Umm."

"I hope David is."

And as we made our way down those spiral stone

stairs, for the last time I hoped, I couldn't help remembering that David had not seemed pleased at all.

SIX

We discovered them in the Pink Lounge. David held the floor, and his explanation to Clarice was given in a crisp and unemotional voice, when you'd have expected more triumph, if only restrained. Clarice was standing by the fireplace, as though she'd sensed something in the way of a revelation, but that the actual details of Konrad's end she found chilling. Though, of course, up to that moment there had been perhaps a slight chance that . . . no, of course he had to be dead, and she had known it. But her dark eyes were watching David's face with intensity.

Anthony was, for once, serious. When George and I arrived, David was well into it, and Anthony still stood by his hi-fi with a hand full of sleeves, but he put them down with an impatient gesture and, unthinkingly it seemed, wandered over and sat on the arm of the easy chair in which Amaryllis sat bunched and withdrawn, her face white and her fingers interlocked.

Anthony said once: "Get on with it!" But it was background noise, and evidence only that he was way ahead of David's reasoning.

"And so," said David, "we've got at least a logical explanation of what happened, though it's not for us to make decisions. But I'll see the police, so that it can all be presented to the inquest jury . . ."

"I'm not having it!" shouted Fisher. "Who the hell're you to say it was this way or that way? Give me time, and I'll knock the whole thing to pieces."

"As I said," David ploughed on, "it'll be up to the inquest jury, who'll of course take note of any other evidence our friend Fisher likes to present. And when they've examined Konrad's drawings and seen the cabinet—"

"They've what!" burst out Sundry. He, too, had been silent. Now he moved towards David with ruffled anger. "You can't hand over that stuff to the police. It's the property of the Magic Circle. Konrad would never . . ."

"Konrad doesn't have much say in it."

"Then, on his behalf, I protest."

"Neither do you," said David flatly. "This is a police matter. There's been a fatal accident."

Fisher bounced in again. "Not an accident. No!"

Then for a few moments there was pandemonium, though Anthony, at least, was quietly amused. He glanced down at Amaryllis, and his face became stiff. Suddenly he was on his feet.

"Be quiet!" he shouted. "What the hell's this

supposed to be—a fish market?"

There was silence, and I thought Sundry looked embarrassed. I moved to David's elbow and he looked at me for one moment. I was shocked at what I saw. "David!" I whispered.

"It's all right, love."

And Fisher intruded into what had been a purely personal remark.

"It's not bloody well all right."

Then I realised that George had moved past me. I had an impression of tight, controlled anger. He took Fisher by both elbows and lifted him bodily, until their faces were close, and spoke quite politely, considering.

"Be silent, little man. And . . . sit . . . there."

He tossed him accurately into an empty chair, and for some reason Amaryllis rushed over to comfort him.

George shook himself, freeing his shoulders from the slight burden. He had gained the attention, and perhaps this had been his intention. He scowled around the room, thrust his hands into his trousers pockets—not trusting them, I suppose—and spoke with an angry growl.

"But it's not all right. Dave's too soddin' polite, it seems to me. He ain't getting round to it. But me, I don't mind saying it. So you're all just going to listen to me for a few minutes. And that goes for you too, Dave."

"Just as you wish," said David, and he reached for his pipe.

"Right. So now we're all nice and quiet. Let's look at what we've got. Here's Dave come up with a nice little theory, which goes along neatly with the double-indemnity part of the insurance. No, damn you . . ." He turned on Anthony, who'd only made a protesting gesture, and he was positively snarling. "Keep *out* of it.

Let me say it and get it over with. Because this was what the great Konrad Klimax was always boasting, that he was worth more dead than alive. Which happens to be absolutely true. He was fading. Nobody wanted him. And his newest illusion turned out to be . . . what? A load of old-fashioned rubbish he could never use. And why was it like that? Because he intended to use it for only one very special illusion—his last. The whole bloody thing was meant to lead right to where we are now. You can't tell me he genuinely expected to use that blasted cabinet in front of the public. Don't make me laugh. *This* was his illusion, that he died by accident, shoved out of the window by his cabinet. Out of a window that was conveniently open on a cold and windy night! Codswallop!"

"Now really . . ." Sundry was looking worriedly at Clarice, who indeed seemed as though she was about to faint. I didn't know how I looked. I felt sick at the implications.

David drew on his pipe, put back his head, and blew smoke at the ceiling. I locked my hand in his arm.

But George was going well now. His voice was rising in anger. "And all he needed was a bright investigator to produce it out of a hat. That'd be so much better than making it too obvious. Maybe he didn't bank on two—one of 'em not so simple as the other . . ."

David grinned, glancing down at me to see whether I shared the joke. And frowned.

"And maybe . . ." George's voice fell to a growl. "Maybe it all seemed much more natural if the investigator could be brought into it by way of his wife, so that it'd be a friendly gesture, not too official. By God, I don't like the smell of that. If Elsa's been—"

Clarice gave a choking cry. Her fingers fluttered and her eyes reached for me. I'd have gone to her, but

David reached over his free hand and trapped mine, and I was glad of it, because my knees felt weak.

"Stop him, David." Because there had to be more.

"No, love."

"Every damn thing you look at leads to it," George claimed. "The failures he kept having. That'd give him the background for throwing the dummy out as a habit, and for stumbling in his anger . . . Oh, Christ, the picture's so clear. His greatest illusion—how to defraud the insurance company of 200,000 quid."

"Oh, yes, yes," cried Fisher, clasping his hands in delight, only now realising exactly what it meant to him.

"No!" Clarice was choking. Auden took her arm, but she shook him off.

"And of course," George grumbled, not liking this at all, "it would have to be done with the connivance of his wife."

This was too much. I tore myself free of David and rushed at George. I suppose I was going to hammer uselessly at his great chest, but he caught my arms, so gently that I felt only the restraint, and through my tears I could see only that round, flabby face of his with the eyes so kind and so soft . . .

"Elsa, please," he whispered. "It's not all."

"It's enough, George," said David softly, taking me easily. Then he turned and raised his voice. "Somebody'd better call the police."

Because it was getting out of hand? Because there was going to be violence?

"I've done that," said Anthony easily. When we stared at him: "I did it when the shouting started."

"So now, perhaps, we wait," David suggested. "We've all got things to think about."

"I don't have to think," said Fisher, nodding, his

eyes bright.

Clarice, who was now sitting with her face in her hands, lifted her eyes for one moment with a glance indicating that any friendship there had been between herself and Fisher was buried, deep. Anthony, seeing this, turned on Fisher savagely, but I missed the rest because David put his arms round me and led me to a seat at the other end of the room, and he was so tender that I became completely incapable of anything for a few minutes.

When I lifted my head David and George were in conference. In dispute, rather. David waved a finger beneath George's nose, only to have it thrust aside. Angrily, David turned and walked away, back to me.

"He's hopeless."

I knew, then, that there was worse to come.

George stood isolated. Apart from Fisher, who was severely suppressing it, there was not one person in sympathy with him. Well, one. I couldn't forget his eyes. My heart went out to him.

"David says wait," he said in a flat voice. "But what's the point? Have it out, that's what I always say. You've just got to take the idea a step further. There's this Konrad, going to make his widow rich, with the best illusion he ever thought up. D'you think he'd leave it all behind? Not on your life. He'd want a share in it. He'd want to share it *with* her. So . . . you can't imagine he'd actually go out of that window. Not a clever chap like him. There'd be another illusion involved, somewhere. And that's the illusion—that he died at all."

"By God, but you're crazy," said Anthony, his voice slurred with contempt. "How the hell could he have got out of there, except through the window? Don't say he climbed . . ."

"I'm not saying that. I'm saying she would have to have worked it with him, simply because she was the one who'd pick up the money. Don't ask me how it was worked—this has all been sprung on us and there hasn't been time to think. But if you want a suggestion . . . Well, have you noticed the height of that room? It was night. Those lamps hang from open joists, a good four feet from the ceiling. He could've been up there, hiding above the light, perched on one of the joists. Of course, he couldn't have stayed up there long. He'd need to have the room empty soon after you got in. And who made sure it was? Who collapsed and had to be taken to her room? Then he could slip out quietly, leaving the illusion intact—and probably head straight for South America . . . Just a suggestion, you understand, but it fits, it fits."

I heard the car in the drive. Time had slipped away. There was none left for retrieval, and George's suggestion hung heavy in the room.

Then the doorbell rang.

Anthony looked surprised, and hurried out.

There was silence. George lifted his shoulders and waited.

"Clarice," said Anthony, re-entering, "here's Inspector Clerihew again."

I think I realised, then, that this visit was not in response to the phone-call. It was this uniformed officer who had first visited the castle when Konrad disappeared.

"Mrs Klein . . ."

He looked round. Inspector Clerihew was probably the most softly-spoken policeman I had ever met. Apart from David, of course, who had been one. Now Clerihew was puzzled, obviously sensing the atmosphere.

"A word . . . alone . . ."

Clarice lifted her head. "No." She repeated it, suddenly bitter. "No. These people know all my affairs. Better even than I do."

"Very well. I have to tell you, then, that your husband's body has been recovered, washed up 20 miles from here, at . . ."

Then she was screaming, her face livid, and the sound tore into my nerves until I had to press my hands over my ears, and allow myself to sink down and down . . .

SEVEN

"What're you doing?" David asked.

I didn't turn. "Packing." I paused. "Of course."

Then I felt his arm round my waist and his chin in the curve of my neck. "But why?" he whispered.

The trouble was that I couldn't be sure. I was completely emotionally confused. My embarrassment was partly for George—and for myself in that I had brought him to the castle—because of his forthright condemnation of Clarice. I could excuse him, because his anger had been on my behalf, but I was not certain how much of his theory could now be accepted. If there was any at all, I felt I simply could not face Clarice. So, feeling out David's own reaction, I simply said:

"That must be obvious."

"She's very upset. I understand she's gone to her room, and Sundry says he can hear her weeping."

"Then he should go in and comfort her."

"I'm sure he would, but she won't let him in."

I turned into his arms and his hand ran up through my hair. Suddenly I was weeping myself.

"David, how *could* she! My friend . . ."

"It's what friends are for," he murmured. "To call on, in case of need."

"If she'd only confided in me."

"Oh, come on now, Elsa. Can you imagine her saying it . . . Elsa, I want you to help me defraud the insurance company, and if you'll phone that big, handsome husband of yours . . ."

So there was no doubt what David thought. "She never called you handsome to my face!"

He was laughing gently. I withdrew my head a few inches to stare at him. "It's not funny, David."

"Of course not, love. But she needs you now, more even than she did then."

"But she deceived me! Her friend! I could tear her hair out."

I shrugged away from him. Sometimes he doesn't understand a thing. To tell the truth, I could not understand my own sudden anger.

"No, you couldn't, you'd simply like to punish her a little. Which you'd do by going to her now and helping her."

"Oh . . . really . . ."

"She'll be ashamed, desperately afraid of facing you . . . and you'd punish her by comforting her."

"It'd be hypocritical."

"Yes, but better than running away. It's always like

this, Elsa. There comes a time when things are being revealed that you'd rather not know, and you want to turn and run. That's when you have to go on."

I considered him carefully from behind my hair, never having realised that his cases could affect him. He himself seemed hurt, and his eyes were unhappy.

"If you want me to, David."

"Of course I do."

I tried to smile. "Then I will."

He laughed, turning away, no doubt to return to the fray. "Good girl." He paused. "Besides, how else will we know how she's taking it?"

I called out angrily after him, but he had closed the door. Then I had a few moments to realise that he was teasing me, a few minutes to tidy myself, then I went along to see Clarice, wondering how she was taking it.

The castle was quiet. I hung over the hand-carved rail of the Gallery, and was unable to decide whether the police were still there. David had told them what he believed had happened, but George had remained silent, his part of the theory now in serious doubt. I believed that David had taken the inspector to the laboratory, to demonstrate, but that seemed to be hours before. Now there was silence.

I turned, and realised that Auden Sundry had been watching me with anxious misery. He was standing outside Clarice's door.

"She will not open the door to me," he said numbly.

Poor man. I said he should give her time. I told him he ought to go down and get himself a drink; he looked as though he needed something.

"I'll see if she'll open up for me," I told him. "I wouldn't let her see you."

Quietly he withdrew. I waited until he was halfway down the Grand Staircase, then knocked.

A pause. "Who is it?"

"It's Elsa."

A longer pause. I was about to speak again when I heard the latch click, and the door opened. "Come in." And she headed back to the bed.

She had been sitting up against the pillows in her slip, her hair disordered and her eyes swollen. She had a tight ball of wet handkerchief in her left hand. I went and sat on the edge of the bed.

"Oh, that terrible man," she moaned, her voice very weak.

For a moment I couldn't think who she meant; there was quite a choice. "You mean George?"

"Saying such horrible things! I shall have to ask him to leave. I suppose he could have gone already . . ."

"I don't think so. You mustn't blame him too much. He was angry for me—for what he suspected."

"Why should he be? David wasn't."

"David knows you're my friend, Clarice."

She thought about that. I was remembering that David's anger had been just as real, but quieter and more contained. At last she nodded.

"Of course. He would never believe such nonsense."

"But George is *his* friend, and if George goes, David will."

"Oh, men are so ridiculous!"

"And I should feel so lonely without him."

"You'd stay with me, Elsa?"

"Of course. As long as you like."

Then she was in tears again, sobbing and snuffling, and throwing herself about with grief. I felt helpless. I could only keep saying, "There, there," and patting her hand. I wondered why Amaryllis had not come to her. After all these years they must surely have been closer than Clarice and me. She seemed to read my thoughts.

"I've been so lonely here, Elsa," she muttered, a little more recovered now.

"But surely . . ."

"Konrad was such a severe man. Devoted, you understand, but not to me. He lived for his illusions. Sometimes it seemed I didn't exist, and of course she was always with him at those times."

"A professional relationship," I said comfortingly.

"Professional my eye! That little bitch flaunted him in front of me. I could have . . ." And she crumpled again.

I tried, really I did. "Could have killed her?" I suggested, making light of it, and wondering whether she'd been about to say: killed him.

"Thrown her out on her neck," said Clarice. "She came at first as a house-guest, but she stayed and stayed, and then Konrad said he needed her here, to turn to . . . How *could* he! But now . . ."

She stared at me past the knuckles pressed hard against her cheeks, and her eyes brightened, then became hard.

"But now I can throw her out."

"Do you think you should?" I asked tentatively. "Anthony might object."

"Anthony? Anthony might? Whatever are you talking about, Elsa? But you're right, of course. A decent interval, then it's out. On her neck."

I glanced at my watch. The time! But she now seemed much more reasonable. "You really must get yourself tidied up, Clarice. You'll want to come down to dinner . . ."

Then she was distraught again. She couldn't face such an ordeal, and would I arrange for a tray, and please, please, not let Amaryllis bring it up!

Dinner, naturally, was miserable that evening. Sundry could think of nothing to say but that he'd leave there and then, but he wasn't leaving until he had the documents for his archives. Nobody listened, and David avoided my eyes. Fisher attempted to draw George into conversation, his friendship a carry-over from what had seemed to be George's support.

But George wasn't supporting anybody at that time. He was heavily morose, and when he caught my eye it was in mute appeal. I tried to smile him out of it, but caught Amaryllis eyeing us with speculation, and returned my eyes to my plate, suddenly desperately uneasy.

After dinner Anthony left without a word, and when I went out into the hall I could hear his music going. *La Boutique Fantasque*. Amaryllis swept past me, her lips tight and her eyes blazing. I watched her to the door of the Pink Lounge, heard it slam violently after her, then the scream of the tone arm being swept from the record.

David said: "You coming up, love?"

"To bed? It's early."

"Our friend Fisher wants to make a demonstration in the Tower."

Fisher would have had to do something for his company. I'd hoped never to enter that room again, but failing that—and I had to have company—it would have to be Clarice.

"If you think it matters," I said without enthusiasm.

"From what he hinted I'm sure it does."

"I'll have to get something warm for my shoulders, then."

He nodded. George said: "I'll wait for her, Dave." David looked at him silently for a moment, then nodded. Then we moved in opposite directions, David and Fisher towards the Tower doorway, George and I to my room.

I had expected some sort of apology, and didn't relish this from George. He was sensitive enough to realise that I understood what he had done, and why he had done it. No apology was needed. If anything, I should have thanked him for his consideration.

He followed me into the room and stood awkwardly as I searched the drawers for my cashmere scarf; incongruous over the shoulders of that dress, but practical.

At last: "Dave says you're not leaving, Elsa."

So David had told him I had intended to. "No. I did think . . . No, we'll have to stay."

"I wish you'd take him away."

I looked at him in surprise. "Do you want to go on alone, George? Is that it? But David wouldn't like that."

"He'd go if you asked him."

"I expect so. But I can't see why."

"These are friends of yours."

"Clarice is."

"You were here a week before it happened. They've all been here, and something must have grown . . . You know what I mean. It's too close. David can't think straight. It's too personal for him."

It didn't sound right. I was willing to bet that George wasn't usually concerned about David's objectivity. And I did not believe that David would be influenced to a great extent, anyway.

"It's this place, George. It makes you feel morbid. We may have to wait around here for the inquest, but I can't see . . ."

"It hasn't finished."

"Don't be such a gloomy old pessimist, George."

He grinned, took my elbow, and led me out on to the Gallery.

"Then stay. I'll need you, if Dave doesn't." Then he was serious again. "I know what Fisher's going to demonstrate. I've watched him playing with it. Oh, he thinks he's doing grand for his company, and I suppose he gets a percentage for every claim he punctures. But that Fisher, he doesn't see farther than what he happens to be doing at the moment."

I paused to take up one of the oil-lamps from the occasional tables along the Gallery.

"It's all right," he said. "I've got a torch."

"What were you getting at?"

"What Fisher does—it's going to lead on to something else. Dave's going to have to say some unpleasant things. But if you took him away, Elsa, then I'd do it."

"Do you want to?"

As we mounted the staircase he kept the torch's beam carefully on the steps just in front of me.

"I don't like these people. There's nothing but deception from every one of them. I don't trust myself with this lot, I'll tell you that. I'm already regretting a few things I've had to say, and I'd prefer not to get involved with any more."

So very formal, for George. But he's the solid, bull-headed type, at home with a bunch of uncomplicated and honest crooks. I could see how he'd hate the convolutions of pretence and deception that were constricting him here.

"George, you idiot, we all love you," I said inadequately.

Then he leaned past me and opened the door.

The laboratory room was much as it had been, the lights on but the window shut. Without realising it, I glanced up into the shadows beyond the hooded lights, then turned in guilt to face George's embarrassed smile.

"It wasn't perhaps a very good idea," he admitted, shaking his head heavily.

I smiled at him, and he seemed more relaxed. David waved a hand towards me in greeting, and Fisher lifted his head and frowned. Perhaps it was supposed to be a men-only party.

They had the cabinet in the exact centre of the room, halfway between door and window. It stood with its door facing me when I entered. Fisher was manhandling a dummy of his own, which seemed to have been made out of two of those from the cupboard.

"It seemed to me," he said, "seeing we're talking about Konrad being in this cabinet, and being thrown out of it through the window by the mechanism, then we ought to work with a dummy of about his weight."

"But we're not." David spoke kindly. "Talking about it in that way, I mean. Not any more. It was a theory that doesn't seem all that valid now we know he's dead."

For a moment Fisher was worried by this inverted reasoning, but he at once recovered, and was belligerent. "Then why were you in that room with the inspector so long? Why's he taken charge of the drawings? You've been brainwashing him, that's what."

"Brainwashing Clerihew?" David grinned. "A lot of chance I'd have of doing that. He listens and nods, but he doesn't accept a word."

"It's quite unethical," Fisher claimed. "Undue influence."

"Get on with it," George growled.

Fisher nodded. He was flushed. "Yes. Well . . . this dummy, it's around Konrad's weight, which is about 200 pounds. You know how heavy this cabinet is? Around 200 pounds as well. So it's equal masses. You follow me?"

"Ahead," said David gravely. "You seem to be handling this apparatus quite competantly."

"I've tried it a dozen times. It always does the same thing."

"Never fails," said George. "Well now, fancy that. But it failed that night. The bullet met *something* inside the cabinet."

Fisher paused, staring from one to the other of them. "I know what you're doing. You're trying to disrupt this demonstration."

"No, no," David protested. "You go ahead."

"All right. Then let's have some attention. I worked this out by theory. It struck me that if a weight of 200 pounds threw out a weight of 200 pounds, then the recoil of the first weight ought to equal the thrust applied to the second. So I tried it. Now watch what happens. Dummy inside, cabinet door open. In your theory, Konrad had stumbled inside. That's him, there. The door's open, and we tilt the cabinet backwards, as you said it did." He slowly tilted it. "Watch."

What happened was that there came a point when the cabinet was leaning back about 20 degrees, and its door flapped wide open.

"That's one possibility," said Fisher complacently. He restored the cabinet to the vertical. "Reduces the chances to 50-50. So we try it again with the door not quite so far open."

Slowly he again tilted it towards the window.

"Notice," he said, "that it's still resting on the back

two castors. It has to be nearly horizontal before the architrave actually touches the floor. Now . . ."

As he removed his hand from the cabinet the door snapped shut. The dummy shot out of the top as the cabinet fell backwards, but the cabinet itself moved back on its castors to crash against the door, and the dummy was deposited with a dismal flop in the centre of the room.

David looked at it with a kind of stolid disappointment. "You say it's done this before?"

"Every time I tried it."

"Hmm! George?"

But George had no comment to make. He shrugged. Fisher seemed disappointed at the reaction. Perhaps he'd expected gnashing teeth.

"So you see, he couldn't have been thrown out of the window by the cabinet." They stared down at it. "And, anyway," went on Fisher forcefully, "that window's so narrow that it's 1,000 to 1 against him actually going through it."

George slapped him on the back in admiration. David said: "Very good reasoning. Who's going to tell her?"

"What?"

"Well, it'd be bad enough for her to have her husband die in order to prove he's worth more dead than alive. Who's going to tell her you've just put the kibosh on her claim?"

"Oh."

"I know what we'll do." David put his arm round his shoulders. "We'll get 'em all together again, and you can do a nice tidy explanation bit, like I did."

"Well . . . I don't know."

"George, give me a hand with shifting this thing."

He and George lifted the top of the cabinet and got

it back on its castors. They slid it to one side so that we could get out. David urged Fisher in front of him.

"Elsa can go and persuade Clarice to come down. We'll do it in the lounge again."

"David, don't ask me to . . ."

I was behind him on the stairs, George following with his torch. David turned, and perhaps it was just the way the light caught his eye, but something there silenced me.

So we descended, with David encouraging Fisher, and every second Fisher becoming more reluctant. I felt uneasy. David, in his heavily flippant mood, is difficult to deflect.

When we'd reached the Long Gallery again, it was all arranged, and I couldn't help being swept along with it.

"You fetch Clarice, love," David told me.

"Really, I couldn't . . ."

"Tell her she'll hear something to her disadvantage."

"I could kill you," I whispered.

But his eyes were bleak. "Get her there, Elsa, some way or other."

So they went on down the staircase. I wished I understood. George looked back, saw me hovering, and returned.

"She's got to know, Elsa."

"Then why can't I just tell her? Oh, George . . ."

"Believe me, this is the best way."

He remained outside while I tapped on Clarice's door, then entered her room. She had been asleep, fitfully. I told her that Fisher was doing things to block her claim to the double-indemnity. She groaned. Really, she looked desperately ill.

"I do think you should come down, and at least be

there."

"I don't want to hear."

"But you have to."

I got her out of bed and into a thick dressing-gown, and helped her through the door. I could feel her shaking. George took her other arm. We led her downstairs. She was protesting still, that I hadn't given her time to do her hair, that I hadn't . . . Her eyes lifted to mine, and they were stunned with misery.

They were all gathered there again, Amaryllis nervously impatient and Sundry on his high horse, his nerves apparently on edge from his interview with Clerihew. He tried to take Clarice's arm, but she stared at him, and he retreated.

Anthony was just plain angry. "I hope this isn't going to take long. We're all very tired."

David wandered towards the centre of the room. He looked round apologetically.

"Martin's asked me to be his spokesman," he explained. "Though I don't really know how to put it. To explain bluntly, he's just demonstrated that Konrad couldn't possibly have been thrown through the window by his cabinet. And so . . ." He gave one of his charming smiles, which bounced bluntly against their combined hostility. ". . . well, I was wrong."

"It's a fine time—" began Anthony.

"Though, in practice, it'd perhaps have been better if Martin had kept quiet about it." David rubbed his hand around the back of his neck. "Shall we say he got carried away! What we've got to realise, here, is that it didn't actually *need* to work, this idea of mine. Not from Konrad's point of view. What he was creating was an illusion, which was that the cabinet had hurled him, by accident, through the window. Probably he hadn't reckoned on Martin being so clever and destroying that illusion, but you see, whether it could actually have happened or not isn't the point. He intended simply that it would be accepted that it had."

There was a sudden outburst of voices, some angry, some protesting. He calmly waited for it to die down.

"George was putting forward an idea that Konrad's illusion had to need the connivance of his wife. We've rather forgotten that, because at that time we heard that he was dead. But, unfortunately, it's still valid. I'm sorry to have to say this, but I wanted Clarice here especially to make the point. Who's going to deny that she's absolutely shattered by the news that Konrad is dead? By that news! Not before, mind you, when everybody here knew that he had to be dead."

"Oh, David!" I whispered, really to myself. But he heard, and his eyes shot to mine, and he shook his head. The pain in his eyes blinded me.

"I'm very sorry about this," he went on. "It really does indicate that prior to that announcement, when everybody else assumed he was dead, Clarice must have believed Konrad was alive."

"Oh, no!" she groaned.

He did not pause. "So Martin has really proved something very basic for us. He's shown us that Konrad's cabinet—his illusion with it—which was to have left him alive while apparently causing his death, couldn't have killed him after all, by accident or in any other way. But . . . he *is* dead. It leaves us in an awkward position, you see. I mean, after all that careful preparation of his, we can't accept that he really did take his own life. And if a different accident happened, one that came to him all unexpected, so to speak—then that'd be too big a coincidence for *me* to swallow, anyway. And, unfortunately, if we dismiss suicide, and dismiss either a prepared accident or an unprepared one, then we've only got one thing left. And that's murder."

David really was apologising. You'd have thought he had done it himself.

For a moment there was complete silence. I heard a sound behind me, a small snapping sound, and turned. Inspector Clerihew was standing quietly in the doorway, at his shoulder his sergeant, who had just snapped his pencil.

I think we had all assumed that Clerihew had left. But then I saw that he was neither surprised nor intrigued by David's conclusion, and it was clear that he already knew. In that event, he had no doubt been busy around the castle with his inspectorial duties.

He pursed his lips and stared at David, who had recovered and was grinning, reaching for his pipe.

"I don't remember," said Clerihew severely, "telling anybody that he was shot."

EIGHT

They held a conference in our room, David and George, even though, by the time we got there, I was very nearly asleep on my feet. But clearly I could not undress and retire with George sitting on the foot of my bed.

David had fastened on to one basic fact—that a bullet had been fired into that cabinet, and had been stopped by something.

"But there was no blood," said George. "In the cabinet, I mean."

"I wonder how long it took the police to get there. With the room empty, the cabinet could have been cleaned out."

"Twenty minutes," I said wearily.

"Well . . . it's possible."

But George was shaking his head doubtfully. "And if he was shot, Dave, how did his murderer get out of the room and leave the cabinet where it was?"

"We've seen how it could have got there."

"But then he couldn't get out."

And so on . . . and so on. Round and round it.

"Shall we sleep on it?" I suggested, and they decided to go up there again and search for inspiration.

This time they could go alone. I reckoned I would have time to undress and get into bed, and probably get a couple of hours in before they got back. But I was half undressed when they banged in again, after only five minutes, and I had to dive behind the open wardrobe door.

"They've put a guard on it!" said David in disgust.

As they would have to, now that murder was common knowledge. I peeped round the edge. "So there's nothing you can do tonight?"

And blessedly there was not. George went to his room, and I thought we would be able to get some sleep at last, but David prowled the room in his pyjamas and smoked into the small hours. Small comfort he was, too, when he did join me.

I did not think I could possibly face the following day. Breakfast was completely disorganised, and any sort of timetable had been abandoned. Before I got down—and David had eaten and disappeared when I did so—a squad of detectives had taken over, and now the atmosphere was more formal, and suspicion hovered like a threatening ghost.

Sundry was playing around with a dish of corn-flakes. "I'm told I can't leave," he grumbled.

"It's always the same. Could I have the coffee,

please?"

"She's been down, you know. Magnificent woman—as firm as a rock this morning."

"Well, yes. Clarice has a strong will. I knew she'd recover." Then I allowed a touch of bitchiness to creep in—I was very tired, I suppose. "After all, now it's officially murder, she can at least depend on £100,000."

He looked hurt. I was about to apologise until I realised he hadn't even heard.

"She wouldn't say a word to me."

Then Fisher came in, and it was clear from his clothes that he had been outside, and judging by his huge scarf, that it was colder.

"If you stand on the battlements," he said, "you can see the whole face of the tower. And it's quite obvious that you'd need a mountaineer with ropes to get out of that window . . ."

"What the hell're you babbling about?" Sundry demanded shortly.

"They talk of murder. It's ridiculous."

A hundred thousand times ridiculous, I thought.

"How could any murderer get out?" Fisher demanded. He had stripped off his outer clothes and was helping himself heartily to bacon and eggs. The fresh air had no doubt given him an appetite; the problem of murder was apparently academic.

But how could he be so naive! Was he still trying to prove suicide? The man was obsessed.

"Don't be ridiculous," said Sundry with contempt.

I decided I'd had enough breakfast, and quietly slid away. David had to be somewhere, and I eventually found him with George in the Cleric's Library, where they were playing with a couple of books, perching them and toppling them, and arguing heatedly.

Anthony followed me in. "I reckoned you had to be here," he said, and they looked at him with interest. I did too.

It occurred to me that I had not seen Anthony sneer for quite a long while. Whatever this sudden death had done to other people it seemed to have steadied him. Anthony was more mature, more dignified, more . . . well, like his father. And whatever the disputes between Konrad and Anthony, they had been, basically, much alike in their work. Konrad used all the stage, the illusion being to distract attention from one side while something happened the other; Anthony used two hands, so that the illusion was simply more concentrated. But their arts were alike. Konrad conducted a full orchestra, while the others performed. Anthony played solo piano, with supreme artistry. Apart, each would be perfect. But . . . a piano concerto? Perhaps not.

"Clarice has asked me to have a word with you," said Anthony calmly. "As you've achieved nothing, and as the police now have things in hand, she thinks you should leave."

David considered him with interest. "*She* says that?"

"Her exact words."

"Though paraphrased, perhaps. But we can't leave. The police would object."

"Nonsense. You weren't even here when he died."

"But Elsa was."

I drew in a quick breath. "But you can't—"

"No. But the police do. You're a suspect, Elsa. And here's the man to tell you."

The young man who stolled in might have been an executive, on the financial side perhaps, of an international combine. He was tall and slim, and had a diffident air, and his eyes were the purest, brightest brown I had ever seen.

"This is Detective Chief Inspector Abel," David said in introduction.

Then I realised that Abel was not as young as he seemed; it was simply that the harrowing nature of his employment had slid past him, leaving no mark, his skin being tough enough to deflect it. When he spoke it was with grave humour—intended as such—but his eyes did not light with it.

"Indeed, she has been. A central suspect. But I hadn't seen her, of course." He gave a formal, mocking bow. "I'm looking forward to taking your statement, Mrs Mallin, and yes . . ." turning to Anthony, his voice cooling. ". . . yes, I forbid her to leave."

"My stepmother is quite distressed."

"I'm sorry to hear that. She would be, of course. But Mrs Mallin remains."

Then Fisher, oblivious to anything other than his own central obsession, burst into the room and made straight for David and George, apparently not even seeing Abel.

"They say he was shot. They *say* that. But he'd been bounced around in the sea for nearly a week. And you've seen those rocks! The body'd be in a hell of a mess, so how'd they know he was shot? A bit of a hole in him . . ."

"Shut your stupid mouth," George advised him quietly.

And David politely answered his question. "They'd find the bullet in him."

"The Police Surgeon is positive," drawled Abel, but he was sharp with interest.

"Tcha! Surgeons! What the hell—"

"Who's this?" asked Abel.

"His name's Martin Fisher. He's a claims assessor for

Konrad Klein's insurance company. Naturally, he's interested in the outcome."

"I'm sure he is. Now, sir, I'm the police officer in charge of this investigation. If you've got any information relevant to my inquiries, I'll be glad to have it."

"You bet I have." Fisher eyed Abel with contempt, clearly underestimating him. "These two, here, they've done nothing but obscure the picture . . ."

"I'll hear it in private," said Abel firmly.

Fisher stiffened his shoulders, then turned to the door. George got to his feet. "Fisher!"

They stopped, Fisher and Abel.

"Don't be a damn fool, Martin," said George, with less bite. "Think what you're doing. Your measly percentage isn't important now."

"What percentage? That's all you can talk about."

"You make it too damned obvious, man. Shut up before you go too far."

"I protest—"

"Look," said George. "Go and cool off. The Chief Inspector doesn't want to know."

"Oh, but I do." Abel smiled. His lips moved and his ears moved; there was no more to it than that.

George glanced at David, who shrugged. So George went ahead. "Probably he gets so much per cent of any claim he squashes. That'd be £200,000 for an accident involving Konrad's cabinet, half that for any other death but suicide, and nothing for suicide. Already he's knocked it down from £200,000 to £100,000. Now he's aiming for the jackpot—nothing. What he doesn't realise is . . ."

"I get bloody nothing. There's been no claim."

"Ha!" said George with massive contempt. "What he's forgetting is that there's a murder here, and it's going to occur to somebody that his personal status as a suspect might become more important than his financial one."

George took a deep breath and paused. He was proud of that, and glanced at David for approval. David pursed his lips and nodded, but he wasn't happy.

"You'll pay for this!" cried Fisher. "It's slander."

"Unless," said Abel smoothly, "there's a basis of truth to it."

It was an invitation for George to stick his neck out. George, who's good at that, did so.

"It's a thought—a theory. Try it for size, huh? There's this idiot, here, who happens to be at this place to arrange the new insurance cover on Konrad's latest illusion. He'd have to be let into a few secrets, now wouldn't he, and he wouldn't be happy about the bit where a gun is fired and splinters fly out of the cabinet. But we hear he'd already signed the policy. Maybe he was having second thoughts. I tell you I would. So what's more natural than that he'd go up there and argue it out with the great illusionist himself?"

I'd expected a protest, but Fisher was silent. Then I saw that Abel's fingers were deep in the flesh of his arm. Abel nodded.

George said: "He knew Amaryllis was up there, so there was something going to happen. Suppose that the genius here saw her coming down from the Tower. Suppose she was showing how shaken she was by it all. Suppose he went up to see Konrad, and Konrad laughed at his fears, and said he had so much confidence in his cabinet that *he* would go inside, and Fisher could fire the gun . . ."

"This is preposterous," Fisher bleated, and Abel said: "Go on."

"And supposing Martin agreed. And we know that it'd been failing the last few times. And suppose it failed again, and Martin drilled one neat hole in the cabinet and another in Konrad. Then where'd he be? Just imagine it. Landed with a man he'd just killed, and on top of that he'd recently signed a policy that'd pay the widow £200,000."

And Anthony, imagining it as requested, threw back his head and laughed heartily. Fisher turned his eyes up in outraged protest to Abel. "Are you going to listen to this?"

"I'd like to hear what happened next."

"Well . . . he'd have to do two things—cover himself personally, and squash the insurance claim. He'd accomplish the second by pushing the cabinet against the door and throwing Konrad out of the window, thus making it look like suicide. Unfortunately for him, we read the set-up as showing that Konrad had had an accident, so that Martin had to work like mad to disprove *that*. But now, if he goes on shouting his head off, somebody's going to think that he's trying to prove suicide for some reason that isn't insurance—and that'd be because he killed Konrad himself."

Anthony wasn't laughing any more. It was with genuine interest that he put the question, a split second before I could do so myself.

"Then how did he get out of the room?"

Abel was smiling. Get round that one! He waited.

"I can show you that too," said George.

"Now that," said Abel, "I should like to see."

"Right!"

"Now," said Abel.

"At your service."

"I'm going to play some music," said Anthony, and he walked out.

It was a funny thing, but on the way up the staircase—and I was the trailing end of the cortège—I didn't hear any music begin from the lounge.

I found that I was completely uninterested in watching any more demonstrations, and now, more than before, the thought of that room was depressing. I hung back, deciding to go along to our room and get my coat . . .

David said: "Aren't you coming, Elsa?"

"I'd rather not."

"And miss George making an idiot of himself?"

I smiled at him, weakly, I'm sure, and followed.

There was no talk of a tilted cabinet this time, because there was no longer any suggestion that it had toppled with Konrad inside. But nevertheless George seized it and laid it on its back on the floor, its door upwards.

"Right," he said. "You get it like this, and you shove it up against the door with its castors pushing against it."

This door, by the way, was a great solid three-inch slab of oak, with wrought-iron hinges. The cabinet lay against it in the way it must have been when we ran up to the room.

"So . . . you pick it up," said George, seizing the end that rested against the door and lifting it. This cabinet, mind you, weighed around 200 pounds, and he was lifting half of it, higher and higher, until it was above the top edge of the door. He turned, quite undistressed.

"Then you open the door under it."

He reached down with his left hand, turned the catch up, and opened it, the end of the cabinet meanwhile supported on one hand.

"And you rest the edge of the cabinet on the top of

the door."

He did so. The door was open about 15 inches. George slapped his palms together. "Who's going to slip through?"

Not me! But Abel was of course the main witness, Fisher could not have been expected to prove something against his own interests, and David looked at me blandly. Me it was.

I slipped through the gap gingerly, and George said: "Now grab the latch, Elsa, and slam the door."

I did. It was at first stiff, then swung free, then, when the falling cabinet caught it, it slammed back at me fiercely. The crash from inside was appalling, and in the sudden silence I realised I was alone on those shadowed and frightening stairs, with what could be *anything* just out of sight around the curves in either direction. I hammered on the door, I shouted. I think I panicked a little. And then there was the blessed drag of the cabinet across the floor and I was able to burst inside with the impetus necessary to project myself into David's arms, to realise that the surprise on his face was not at my entrance but at Fisher, who had thrown himself at George in a fury.

It must have been an insane one, because he had just witnessed a display of George's strength. They were easily separated. Abel was affable, even amused.

"Well," he said, "a bit of light relief never hurt anybody. But I wonder who else round here—in the county even—could do what you've just done with that cabinet. Oh, come on, it's quite impracticable. Besides, just look at that door. You've put castor marks all down the bottom half, and there weren't any before."

Fisher was more calm, but the bounce had gone out of him. "He's always chucking around his blasted theories."

"Yes." Abel smoothed his hair, long, silky, blond. "But I already knew that Konrad Klein wasn't shot inside the cabinet."

David reacted. "Then why did you . . ."

"I'm very receptive to ideas, if only to eliminate them. But, you see, there was no blood in the cabinet. And nobody could clean away enough to deceive our pathologist. Also, you see, there was no bullet found inside it, and it's unlikely a murderer would think it of such significance that he'd search for it and take it away."

"Bullet?" said David, all attention. "Why should there have been a bullet if it was in his body?"

"Oh, did I say that? Surely not. There was a clear shot right through the chest. Front to back—missed the bone everywhere. And just think, if he *had* been shot inside the cabinet, it must have been so spent after going through his body that it failed to go through the opposite panel, or even make a mark on it."

He smiled complacently and patted Fisher affably on the shoulder. "So you see, you didn't have to get all worked up."

I could see that this casually offered information meant a great deal to David. His eyes met mine, and his were completely out of focus. It was as though he groped for my support in something, but I could only grasp his arm. His muscles were tense.

But somehow I sensed what he was thinking; that his original theory was basically correct, and the set-up was a cover for Konrad's faked death by accident—but something different had occurred, though not what George had propounded. And because of its apparent impossibility I felt the skin prickle down my spine, and David glanced at me when I shuddered.

Then the door opened slowly, and we all turned to look at it. Clarice entered, Amaryllis at her shoulder. They were both looking very frightened. "We heard the bang."

"Ah!" Abel almost opened his arms to them. "You came at a very appropriate time."

I couldn't see what was appropriate about it.

"If you would sit down," he suggested to Clarice.

Chairs? I'd seen no chairs. But there was one, an upright. Clarice almost collapsed into it, with that action transforming the scene into something like an inquisition, she being the only one seated.

"I've been thinking," Abel began quietly enough, "about the idea that David Mallin put forward. You remember: that your husband faked an accident with this cabinet in order to defraud the insurance company?"

But David had not said that; but he didn't object.

"Yes," Clarice whispered.

"But you've disputed that?"

"Of course."

"No. You disputed the fact that you knew about it."

"I didn't know."

"But you admit it was what he intended?"

She untwined her fingers, twined them again. "It must have been."

"There's no must about it. Do you believe he did?"

"Yes."

"But he'd given you no hint?"

"No."

"What about his claim that he was worth more dead than alive?"

"That was a joke. A lot of men say that."

"I don't."

"But I bet you are," she flashed at him.

He smiled coldly. "I'll have to work it out. So . . . having had no hint . . . his sudden disappearance must have been a shock to you."

"What do you think!"

"Was it not?"

"Of *course* it was."

"Particularly as he could not have left this room alive, the window being the only way out?"

"Yes."

"But tell me—and this has been confirmed over and over—why were you so much more distressed to hear that his body had been found?"

"It was . . . more real. There'd been a chance . . ."

"Nonsense. You invited two inquiry agents here, not to prove he was still alive, or even to discover how he'd died, but to prove the necessary facts for your insurance claim."

"That's not true. I wanted advice."

"But they did, and you were pleased."

"Relieved."

"Until his body turned up."

"The shock . . ."

"When you'd believed him dead already?" his voice was like ice; I hoped he would never speak to me like that. "No, don't look away. You were shocked because you really believed him to be alive, in spite of all the evidence. And you could not have believed that unless you'd worked it with him."

"No!"

"You deliberately left this room empty for him to get free."

"Oh . . . really!"

"You'd join him later and enjoy . . ."

"No, oh no!"

"Yes, oh yes," he blazed at her.

"He's dead!" she screamed. "Isn't that enough for you?"

"No. Not enough. The truth, Mrs Klein. We're talking, now, about complicity to defraud."

She sobbed. Amaryllis touched her shoulder in sympathy. Clarice raised her face, fierce red patches on her cheeks. Yet I thought her eyes were calm, even calculating. But she had nothing to lose, now, nothing. Konrad had been murdered, and nothing was going to alter it.

"He . . . he worked it all out. I didn't approve. But we . . . we were finding it difficult to carry on. I was going to join him, later, when he let me know—with the money. Oh . . . oh, it was clever." She sobbed in bitter amusement at Konrad's cleverness. "But he didn't tell me what he intended . . . just to . . . to rush up when I heard the crash . . ." She glanced up at Amaryllis. "As we heard it a few minutes ago. Oh, dear Lord, but I didn't know, and all I did was what he said."

There was a passionate innocence in her voice, but I could not meet her eyes.

"Which you did to the letter?"

"Exactly what he said. Yes, I did that."

"Knowing he had arranged some means of getting from this room and hiding low somewhere?"

"Believing that."

"I said: knowing. Did he say he was going to do that?"

Her voice became slurred with pain. "He said so. Obviously, he didn't."

"Why obviously?"

"Because he was killed first."

"Before he had a chance of getting to his hideaway, you mean? But didn't you check?"

"How could I? I didn't know where."

"But surely there'd be somewhere, a flat, a cottage . . . something like that, which you both knew."

"Not that I knew."

"Are you telling me he had some private place which was his own secret?"

"It's what I'd assumed."

"*Already* assumed, you mean, before he told you his plans?"

"Well, no." She tossed her head, her hair flying. "Well, yes, damn you, I thought he'd got a woman somewhere."

"Hmm." Abel looked away from her, then back. "A woman, then, with whom he might have intended to leave, after using you to help with the deception . . ."

Her voice cracked. "How could that be, you damn fool, when I'd be the one with the money!"

"Well, yes. How clever of you to have realised that."

"And, obviously, he didn't get to her." She rustled her shoulders in triumph.

"How do you know that?"

Because we all knew who that secret lover was—Amaryllis. And she was there, with us, with no secret flat . . .

"Because he was killed first," she snapped.

"Now there," said Abel, a little hurt I thought, "is where everybody seems to be getting confused. There's absolutely no evidence that Konrad Klein was shot in this room, no blood, no bullet. Only a fired gun, and with logical evidence of where that shot went, and evidence that there was no second one. And it seems certain, now, that he had a prepared method of getting out of an apparently sealed room safely. So why not accept the obvious, that he *did* leave this room alive, and was shot elsewhere? After a week in the sea, a body's so . . ." He coughed, glancing at Clarice. ". . . the medical crew cannot be sure to a day or two, in those circumstances. And so . . . I don't think we need to become too involved with illusions and the like. This is a straightforward shooting. I only wish I knew where it happened."

Which was doubtless why, when he withdrew his team, they left the gun behind.

NINE

I look back at that time as a turning-point, not only with the case—which took on a completely changed aspect—but in personal relationships and my own basic philosophy of life.

Clarice's admission that she had connived in fraud with her husband came as a direct blow to me. This had been a theory only, and I'd been able to thrust it to the back of my mind as unacceptable. But suddenly it was true, that I'd been used and deceived. This fact I found difficult to accommodate emotionally, as it involved a friend. But the really terrible thing was that it was reflected in my own precious relationship with David.

Perhaps I had taken his truthfulness too much for granted. His basic existence had always seemed to rest on a search for truth. But now, having been proved to be too trusting, I found myself watching him for reassuring evidence of its continuing existence, touching his arm to attract the warmth of his smile. I felt like a lost child, and perversely could not live with the uncertainty of the proof, but had to leave him and wander alone for long periods.

At the same time I was aware that David and George were no longer working together as a tight team. David now pursued the emotional side issues for clues, whereas George persisted stubbornly in his idea that Konrad had been killed in that room.

The atmosphere became frigid. Nerves were strained, and no facet of our lives seemed normal. And I realised, bitterly, as one does when apparently excluded from human contact, one of the most dreadful ironies of the situation. Clarice, in finally admitting her shock on hearing that Konrad's body had been found, had sacrificed her friendship with me for the greater glory of innocence of his muder. I wondered how much this admission had been an act too.

This occurred to me much later in the day. Clarice had left with the police to identify Konrad's remains; a gruesome thought. I did not see her return, and deliberately kept my distance so as not to meet her. I put on a coat and went out on to the battlements.

It was cold, and rain like sea spray, it was so salty on my lips, lay moist on my face. The cloud layer was thin and broken, and as the sun set it caught red and gold glints in the frayed edges. I had walked several times all round the castle's perimeter, and then stood in the shelter of one of the smaller towers which marked each change of direction, waiting for the comfort of the sunset's glory, its reliability. I thought of Clarice . . . and became aware of movement farther along the battlements.

I did not deliberately conceal myself, simply stood still. It was a man and a woman. The light was failing, the shadows chasing up the walls. Then they turned, and the flowing sun lit their faces. A skirt flared in the wind and Sundry put up his hand to his hat brim. Their voices were tossed away and a seventh wave crashed high over the rocks, but I could see they were in dispute. He put a hand on her arm, and then, furiously, Clarice whirled on him and I saw his head jerk back with the blow.

I stood. She came past me in a furious whirl, her head high, a scarf held tight over her hair with both fists firm in the silk. When I looked again, fearing he would follow her, there was no sign of Sundry.

I went to tell David. He had spoken to me about possible betrayal. He had said that it was a dangerous thing to fake one's own death and trust to a wife to handle the money, especially one such as Clarice. And he'd said that as she might have a lover around, especially in view of Konrad's own relationship with Amaryllis, then the proceeds might be a fair temptation to make sure the death was not a fake after all.

Well, I could now tell David that the lover was Sundry—or I would have done if I could have found him. George, I knew, was up in the Tower, and David should have been talking intimately with one of the suspects, searching for hints. I couldn't even find the suspects. So, disappointed, I slowly climbed the Grand Staircase, intending to return to my room, and at the point where one's vision reaches above the level of the

Gallery, I paused.

David was just closing behind him the door to Amaryllis's room.

I turned and walked down again. He couldn't have seen me or he would have called my name. Or would he? I walked blindly into the lounge, where Anthony was standing, moody and despondent.

On seeing I was alone he brightened. He sat me down and his personality irradiated me, and I was cold. He ran through a gamut of his conjuring tricks for my entertainment, and I could not respond. He put on a record for me, and grossly parodied his father's illusion of the magic doll—to *La Boutique Fantasque* of all things—and if he expected me to dance the doll he was wildly mistaken . . . And yet, such was the strength of his personality, wildly facetious now, that I did indeed find myself in his arms, and my grotesquely stiff movements might well have been those of a dummy. For some reason he was calling out encouragement in a choked foreign accent, and at last the bizarre humour of it began to flow into my limbs, and I actually found myself moving in an impromptu dance to the beat of the music. I did not notice the door open. I turned only when the scream splintered the mood.

Amaryllis threw herself at Anthony. They went over together in a shattering of minor furniture, Anthony crying out. Her skirts were round her thighs. I ran in to try to separate them, and she turned her face up, distorted with hatred, one arm flinging me away. She was going for his hands, I saw, nails to his eyes so that he naturally protected them, then sinking her teeth in his fingers like a wild animal shaking the kill.

He screamed. Blood spattered her dress. His eyes were all terror, with spittle on his lips. Then he fought one hand free and did the only possible thing, drawing his fist back as far as possible and striking her full in the mouth.

She was unconscious when I reached her. Anthony dragged himself away, and to his feet, his face wild. He was staggering.

"Keep that bitch away from me!"

I smoothed the hair tenderly from her forehead. "Get David," I said.

"Go to hell!" And he slammed out of the room.

She moaned and moved her head. Her lips were split and blood was trickling down her chin. I struggled with her to a settee and managed to lift her onto it. Her eyes opened, glazed, and she said distinctly:

"You bitch! You're not getting away with it."

I turned as the door opened, half rising to my feet. David did not at once notice Amaryllis.

"What's going on, Elsa? He was crying."

"Help me with her, David. She's in shock."

He came and looked down at her. Her eyes cleared. She ran her tongue along her lips and smiled at him. "Hello there."

"She'll be all right," he said.

"She *is* all right, damn her."

She was staring at me. I turned away. "We'll have to get something to bathe her mouth," I said numbly. "Will you fetch it or shall I?"

He reached over to turn me to face him. Amaryllis moved, swinging her feet to the floor. Now her voice was slurred, but rational. "Don't worry, I'll do it myself."

I could only stare at her in indecision, unable to find any enthusiasm. She was not steady on her feet. David helped her to the door. He opened it, and would have helped her all the way up to her room, but her tone was decisive. "Leave me alone. I can manage." We both knew that that was for my benefit.

I sat where she had warmed it and David stood over me.

"Now, what's all this?"

"There was a fight. Anthony—for once—wasn't teasing her. But she went at him . . ."

"That's not what I meant. You, Elsa. Your attitude."

I looked beyond his left ear. "You were in her room."

"I was looking for something."

"I hope you found it."

"No."

"I searched everywhere for you, and couldn't find anybody . . ."

"I saw her go out."

"It didn't seem she'd been out."

"For Christ's sake!" he shouted. "What's the matter with you . . ."

"You were in her room. Looking for something." My voice caught and I couldn't go on.

"I was looking," he said stonily, "for her uniform, her outfit, or whatever you'd call it."

"Oh, yes? Going to stage one of your wonderful reconstructions?"

"Yes, if you like. If you like."

"Oh, not for my benefit, David. Not that."

"She was not there. I searched. I couldn't find it."

I looked at him then, David baffled and angry and hurt. "Then go and ask her now."

"Oh, God." He turned away.

"I'm going up."

"Wait a minute."

I didn't wait because I was uncertain suddenly, and

afraid. I ran out of the room and into George's arms.

"What's this?" he said, sweeping me up. Oh, the glory of those certain arms! "Elsa, you're crying."

He carried me like a child over to David, and in his great naive innocence he offered me to him, grinning, the great baboon, and handed me to my husband.

"I could never handle crying women, Dave. Here."

David took me in his arms, because he couldn't do anything else, and held me tightly against him, but only to hide my distress from George, and I could feel him shaking through and through.

George said: "I was looking for you, Dave. Got something to show you. Come on up."

"We're coming, George."

"Not me," I whispered.

"Oh, yes." Suddenly his voice was light. "Daren't trust you out of my sight. Come on, George, let's see what wonders you've performed."

TEN

I don't know how I managed the stairs, George leading, David behind. George chattered cheerfully. Very sensitive, George is. I owed him a kiss, I decided.

"Eight-inch steps," he said over his shoulder. "I measured 'em. Been measuring everything. D'you know how high that room is? Twelve feet. That's 18 steps to the next floor level, or to the roof if you like, 'cause there's no other window above it. Here we are."

We stopped on the little landing in front of the door to Konrad's room.

"I thought," George said, "that I'd go up on the roof. I mean, we'd got to eliminate all chance of him having a rope hanging from the roof and climbing up there out of the window." He shrugged. "Come on."

We climbed, round and round. You lose touch with direction and height. Then we were standing on another, more extensive, landing. The wall was blank in front of us. Six inches above George's head there was a trapdoor with a huge, rusted—and now broken—padlock hanging from it.

"Not a chance that the trapdoor's been used," said George. "I had to force it—the padlock was rusted solid. Did you count 'em?"

"What?" asked David.

"The steps from the last landing."

"No."

"It's 23, Dave. Should be 18, and that to the roof. So it's five too many, that's over three feet, plus the distance from this landing up to the trapdoor, another seven feet. Ten feet in all. Where'd they go, Dave? There's ten feet not accounted for between the ceiling of Konrad's room and the roof."

"And no window," I offered, feeling a bit better by then.

"Good girl," said George. "Let's go down again."

We did, until he stopped us. There was no landing.

"Took some finding," George admitted. "Disguised, so there's no landing, which'd give the game away. About here, I think. You simply push it—ah, here we are."

A five foot by two foot opening moved away from us, the whole curved surface of stone swinging on hinges. George went first. Total blackness faced us, cut by his torch rays.

"No electricity in here," he called. "Just a sec'."

A flame flickered. He lowered the chimney, and the light of an oil-lamp climbed the walls. We stepped inside, David and I.

The room was smaller than the one beneath us, partly because the curve of the stairs was walled in completely, but it was round, as the other had been. With no window, and the door closed behind us, there was a weird lack of orientation.

The iron bedstead might well have stood at any angle. The table and single chair required no specific relationship to wall or bed. There was a cupboard, storage I supposed, and a spirit stove. I saw crockery, neatly stacked on a shelf, itself incongruously straight against the curved wall. There were no facilities for washing, none for fresh water. A large plastic container could have contained water, but it would probably be stale.

The bed was neat, army style with their sort of blankets firmly tucked in, an uncrushed pillow lying above them at the head.

"His hidey-hole," said George proudly.

The only concession to comfort was a six by three rug with an Axminster weave in dull grey, now completely ruined by a large and irregular stain in its centre.

George said: "It's obvious the place never got used. It was set up for a few miserable days of occupation, but there's not one food packet been opened, and the kettle's never even been boiled."

"He didn't get time," David observed. He dropped on his knee beside the rug, touching the stain tenderly. "Dry now." He stood up. "We'd better call the police."

But George hadn't finished. His eyes were bright, waiting for David's attention. At last he spoke.

"No point in that, Dave. You don't think I'd come running to you like a daft kid as soon as I found it! I've spent two hours in here, searching. But . . . no bullet. And we know the bullet went straight through him. So

. . . where is it?"

"And the shell case?"

"That too." George nodded. "He wasn't shot in here, Dave. He never reached here, for the simple reason that he was killed in his room below."

David seemed annoyed at George's fixation. "We've been through all that. There was no shell case in there either." Then his eyes opened. "No shell case, George, and we know one shot was fired. Into the cabinet."

"Oh!" George was casual. "I found that one." He plunged his hand into his pocket and felt around, finally producing it proudly. "Against the wall, under the dummy Konrad threw there."

"Then how the hell can you say that Konrad was shot down there? We've got that one shell case, with the gun jammed before the second could be fired. And *that* bullet went through the side of the cabinet into the dummy . . ."

"No," said George.

"What?"

"Dave, you don't think I've been wasting my time, do you! It was a theory. It had to be tested out. So I took that dummy apart. And there was no sign of a hole in the suit it was wearing, and no sign of one in its innards. Dave, mate, we've got to start rethinking."

"But, George, for heaven's sake, think now! That bullet was stopped inside the cabinet. Konrad *can't* have been inside. We've got to accept what Abel said about the blood. So what stopped it but the dummy? That's what it was there for, dressed like Amaryllis, to take her place. Talk sense, man. He can't have been shot down there."

"But if he was alive, then he left his room. He didn't get out of the window alive, because he could not have climbed down on to the rocks. OK, Dave? And he can't have climbed on to the roof. And if he managed, somehow, to leave by the door, he couldn't have gone *down* the stairs, because of the chance that he'd have met somebody coming up. So he'd have to come up the stairs, and where else but to here? And, Dave, he wasn't shot here."

"The carpet . . ." I whispered, my stomach queer.

"In spite of the carpet, Elsa," said George firmly.

"So he came here, hid a while, and left—and was shot somewhere else." David was tersely emphatic.

"And didn't even sit down? There's undisturbed dust on the only chair, and the bed coverings are absolutely smooth."

"Tidied . . ." I began, but they both looked at me. It was not a woman we were discussing.

"So . . . what?" asked David. Oh dear, he did sound so depressed.

"He was shot in the room below. The rug was clearly brought here from where he was shot. Not only would it be tricky to get it to here from anywhere but the room below, but if he was shot in that room, it would be necessary to hide that fact. And this is the only place it *could* be brought."

"But, George . . . Oh, Lord, George, then we're back to finding how his murderer got out of there."

"With the rug," he agreed cheerfully.

"Oh, blast you, George!"

"I wonder if anybody's thought of dinner," said George.

ELEVEN

But of course the police had to be contacted. George dutifully performed this task, then headed for the ballroom, and his anticipated meal.

Clarice, apparently, had completely abandoned her duties as hostess, and the salaried help had deserted us, as far away as the police would permit. Amaryllis had firmly shut herself away, which just about left the responsibility to me. Hanging around looking hungry but useless were Sundry and Anthony, who brightened when he saw us approach.

"Martin's doing something in the kitchen," he said.

Both his hands were bandaged. They were clearly causing him pain, and some anxiety, because he kept flexing one with the other. But he had a pale smile for me. Perhaps he was grateful for my small assistance with Amaryllis.

"Something involving a tin of corned beef," he enlarged.

"I'd better go and check."

"Then don't be long." He touched my arm. The sudden intimacy brought a rush of warmth to my cheeks.

When I headed for the door leading to the kitchen quarters, I saw George eyeing me gravely. He moved across, surprisingly quickly for his size, and intercepted me at the door.

"Elsa . . ." George, worried, casts a very large shadow in my life. He shook his head slowly. "Don't ever run from David, Elsa, there's a love."

I remembered the kiss I owed him. He blinked; his eyes flickered. "Promise me," he said gently.

"Promise," I said. "Only in your direction, George."

I heard his laugh through the solid door as I closed it behind me.

There was a long corridor to the echoing tomb they called the kitchen. The actual operations unit of this was in one corner. You could have held a ball in what was left, with room for the Vienna Philharmonic to supply the Strauss waltzes. In the corner Fisher was exercising his skill as a cook by dumping frozen chips into a saucepan of boiling oil. It was going to be chips and cold corned beef.

"There's some tinned rice pudding," he said, though why with pride I couldn't imagine. "Won't take a minute to warm up."

"Entrée?"

"Chop a few melons, my dear. Let's not get too fancy."

I stood by him and watched helplessly. I said: "The two other women aren't coming down. I'd better get trays." Then, as an afterthought: "The police are on their way."

"Again?" He prodded a chip. "The trick is to take it slow till they're soft, then speed up at the end for the crispness. What's happened now?"

I told him, not with all the details, and certainly with none of George's logic.

"Ah, yes," he said quietly, satisfied. "They said he'd have somewhere to hide himself. And naturally it'd have to be close. Clarice knew, of course."

"Now, Martin . . ." I was surprised mainly at his calm triumph.

"You don't think she told the whole truth? Of course she'd know where he meant to hide." He was ladling the chips out with a wire sieve. "And she'd go back there when things were quiet and shoot him herself. I wonder if the policemen would care for a few chips."

"If there's any to spare," I said, my mind racing. "But it was obvious he hadn't been in that room," I whispered.

"Obvious? How long've you got to be here before what's obvious begins to strike you as suspicious? There, that'll do for Clarice. Tell her to get stuck into that. Oh, and remind her—no, *tell* her, because I'm sure she hasn't thought of it—tell her not to count too much on £100,000 for Konrad's murder. We wouldn't pay out to the person who'd done it."

I hadn't said a word about the undented bed, and the idea that a man, having sat on it, would not trouble to tidy it. But Fisher had seemed to be able to read my mind. A man might not—but Clarice would. Heavens, it was just what she'd think about!

I had difficulty with my voice. "I hadn't intended to

visit Clarice."

"Then I will. Here, my dear, take this to Amaryllis."

"I doubt her mouth will take kindly to chips."

"Her mouth?"

So he didn't know. "She's hurt it."

"Then take a double helping of the pudding."

We put covers over the plates. I added a glass to the cutlery and a half bottle of Mouton Cadet, and headed out to the ballroom, on the way to the staircase. Still I could not attempt to speak naturally to David, and registered only that he smiled tentatively at me. But George read my expression. He was at my elbow in a second, saying: "I'll help you with that," as an excuse to get a few minutes with me.

George solemnly marched up the staircase at my side, carrying the tray with one hand, the other at my arm. I was aware that cars were arriving in the drive, many cars. George said:

"Persuade her to come down later, Elsa."

"I don't suppose she'll want to."

"After Abel's gone, Dave's got some idea for a reconstruction."

"Oh, no!" For me? It was taking it too far. "He doesn't need to do that."

"He thinks he does. Short-cutting, he calls it. When Dave gets to trimming the corners it means he's running out of ideas."

He said it absently, his eyes firmly ahead. I glanced at him.

"You know the reason for this, don't you, George?"

"Some theory he's got."

"I mean the *real* reason."

"As I said . . ."

"I'm not going to go along with it."

We stopped at her door. He spoke gently. "You've

never been in on one of his cases, Elsa, not from start to finish. Things are apt to get rough, though usually it's more physical. I can handle that, and Dave's useful when it comes to it. But this one . . . it ain't quite my mark. Nobody to thump. So . . . how's about doing it for me, then, and help get this thing out of the way? I want to get away from this damned place."

I saw that George, for all his eagerness to tackle problems and discover logical answers, was getting very close to being beaten on this one. He looked hurt and troubled.

"I want to get *you* away from here," he said quietly.

I didn't answer. I went in to Amaryllis.

I suppose that these stage people must have a certain resilience. The show must go on, and all that. There must also be professional methods of hiding wounds and disabilities. Or maybe she was possessed of a fierce spirit of self-protection. Whatever it was, the mess of her face, which I'd expected, was not at once apparent. She was not even close to prostrate, but was standing at her window in slacks and sweater, smoking, and whirled on me when the door opened.

"I thought I was going to starve."

"You could have come down," I told her severely. But her lips were thick and one cheek showed a slight welling.

"What's going on?" she asked, gesturing to the window.

"They're here again."

I had put the tray on the table, and whisked off the covers. Somehow, I'd expected anyone as delicate and fragile as a ballet dancer, even an ex-one, to recoil at the sight of chips and corned beef and rice pudding. But no. I reminded myself that ballet dancers had to be all muscle and flexibility, and were probably as tough as all-in wrestlers. She laughed, seeing my expression.

"As recently as six months ago I was touring with Konrad. Things could be pretty rough around the clubs."

"Yes. Yes, I see."

"What do you see?" She picked up a chip, bit it, nodded, and sat at the table. "Have a chip, why don't you!"

"Mine's downstairs. George found Konrad's secret room, you know. Up in the top of the tower."

She was eating competantly enough. "Then the policeman was right. How wonderful to be so handsome and so clever." But she was teasing me, referring to David! "And what," she repeated casually, "do you see?"

I stood and looked down at her bent head. "When you were touring there'd be no difficulty. You and Konrad, together. Thrown together, you might say. But the past six months . . . you were living here. It would be awkward, and rather obvious if you left the castle together for a day or two. There would *have* to be somewhere secret, where you could both go."

She cut me short, looking up at me and laughing, then throwing back her head to make the most of that long neck. "Oh, that's splendid. But he came to me, if he wished—if *I* wished—in my room. Konrad was never one for pretence—"

"He was all pretence."

"Not in his private life, my dear. He was quite outrageous. It was delicious."

"But not recently."

She looked down at her plate. "That Anthony! He thinks he's in love with me. Ridiculous. He's been jealous of his father in his career, and he thinks he's got to carry it over . . ."

"It's no more than that?"

"But Konrad noticed. Lately he'd been cool. I tried to reassure him. But no. Obviously he'd got *this* on his mind, this special illusion of his."

"The illusion of his death?"

"If you like."

"But he didn't confide in you about it?"

"No, he didn't. Won't yours be getting cold?"

"It can wait. Then you didn't know about his secret room?"

She was finishing the wine. The rice pudding didn't meet her approval, it seemed. "Tell me . . ." She pointed the glass at me. "Does it have pink curtains and a luxury bed, and soft lighting, and the facility for sexy music? Does it have a dressing-table I could sit at and make myself beautiful for whatever work he had in mind? Does it have a shower . . ." She laughed at my expression. "Then I wouldn't be interested."

I said: "David wants you to come down later."

"Not me."

"But why not? You seem fit enough."

"Will Anthony be there?"

"I'm sure he will."

"Then no. I could well kill him."

"He wants . . . I understand that what David's got in mind is some sort of reconstruction." I paused. It was difficult to say. "He was thinking of you in your uniform, or whatever you call it, your stage costume."

"Then he's going to be disappointed."

"It did seem important."

"The answer's no."

"Then perhaps I could stand in for you. If you'll get me the outfit . . ."

"You?" She eyed me with something close to

contempt. I admit my figure is fuller—*admit* it, damn it I'm proud of it—but we were much of a height. I stiffened, my cheeks hot. She went on: "You in tights and black pants and a sequined set of tails! My dear, you'd look ridiculous."

But my legs are better. "You shouldn't be afraid of comparisons," I said, condescending a little. "Where is it?" I headed for her huge, wide wardrobe.

"You leave that alone," she snapped, and her eyes were suddenly dangerously bright.

I paused, and looked back at her. "You *are* afraid of comparisons."

"I'll come down," she said savagely.

"Not if it's too much effort."

"Get out of here!" she screamed, and so I left.

I had done as David wished, whatever his reasons. You can't blame me for taking a little pleasure from it. I was smiling when I left the room, and George, hovering, noticed it.

"You managed it?"

"There's no need for you to have waited, George. She'll bring the tray down herself."

"Good girl. David's going to be very pleased."

I didn't reply. I was aware that George's deferring of his meal just to keep an eye on me was a distinct and flattering honour. George, too, was silent; no more moralising.

Amaryllis had spoken almost casually of her abandoned career as a ballet dancer. She had admitted she could not have reached the top. But she was a fighter, not so easily accepting defeat. No . . . her switch to the less legitimate stage had centred on Konrad. From their first meeting he had been able to do anything he wished with her. But now Konrad was gone, and she had nothing. This was what

Anthony meant when he taunted her with her ballet music. He offered her the only future that even showed itself, an alliance with himself. It was a vicious way to do it, though maybe he knew her better than I did. Some women respond to cruelty; some women live by violence.

The air seemed thick with police in casual clothing. Some already nibbled chips from newspapers, which Fisher might have considered appropriate. The printing ink, I understand, gives them a distinctive flavour.

Mine were awaiting me on a plate. David stood and drew back my chair. I murmured something. He told me that Fisher had been entertaining them. Was still doing it, in fact, and had broken off only in politeness until I was settled, though he obviously wasn't pleased to have it described as an entertainment. Because Martin Fisher was hell-bent on his Clarice theory.

I did think they might have kept mine warm; perhaps this is what the newspaper does. The chips were damp and soggy. George, similarly afflicted, swept my plate from under my nose and marched off towards the kitchen, with the awkward result that I had nowhere to concentrate my gaze, and no one had had the kind thought of wine for us, to alleviate the distress.

Sundry was sitting beside Fisher, opposite me, and was clearly suffering from his good manners. Being a trained gentleman he was trying to be polite, but letting it boil up inside him was not a good idea.

". . . she goes up then," Fisher was saying when I began to register again, "and shoots him out of hand. I know that sort of woman, apparently deferring to her husband, but quietly as tough and strong—"

"Mr Mallin believes otherwise," said Sundry softly.

"He hopes to prove that Konrad was shot in his own room."

"Can prove," David murmured.

"Chuff," said Fisher in disgust. "That's a lot of hogwash. The place was sealed off."

"He's promised to demonstrate what he means." Sundry's voice was tight.

David raised his chin. His face seemed more sunken, his eyes, in that light, unhealthily feverish. "I only said I wanted a reconstruction. I thought I could show how he could have been shot by accident. While he was actually using the cabinet, that is. That was all . . ."

"David, please," I whispered.

He turned his dark, worried eyes on me. "I did tell you it was what I wanted."

All was pain. I could see he had to maintain the pretence, for me, and in that way was allowing the conduct of the investigation to become distorted.

"You don't have to do this."

On the face of it he was attempting to go along with George's proof that Konrad had been killed in his room. But there was no conviction in his eyes. Not even when he said:

"I can demonstrate this."

"I don't believe you," I said, and Fisher caught on it in grand triumph. "You see! Even your wife knows that Clarice did it."

"I did not say that." I was firm with him, even angry, but I was becoming completely confused. I didn't know who I was supporting, nor in what. Fortunately, George provided a diversion by banging down in front of me a huge helping of chips, beside which the corned beef had grown by several slices. At least, I could fasten my eyes on it, if only in fascination, and manage to say:

"Amaryllis is coming down later."

"You mentioned the outfit, I suppose?" David asked, not giving an inch.

"I even offered to wear the thing. But she told me my legs weren't good enough." A complete lie; you have to fall back on something.

"I'm not sure I like this idea," Sundry protested gently. "I mean, we could use a dummy . . ."

"No. I want this to be authentic." When David speaks like that there's no appeal. "I want this to be how Konrad planned the illusion. Was it, in other words, an illusion he might seriously have expected to use professionally, or was it something rigged for the one purpose of faking his death?"

"We've had that!" Fisher shouted. "We've heard it all. Clarice admitted as much."

"Yes?" David cocked his head. "Then we'll have to see. What we want to know is what happened, not what he planned. I have in mind . . ."

"What you've got in mind," said Fisher scornfully, "is earning *your* fee, protecting *your* client."

"What I want," ploughed on David resolutely, "is the whole thing, as it would've been on the stage, Amaryllis in full rig, and perhaps Sundry, if he has his tails here—"

"Not me!" Sundry was shaking; his voice was beyond control.

"Then I'll do it myself. Maybe . . ." He glanced round. "Maybe I'm much Konrad's size—I never saw him. Clarice can surely find a spare set of white tie and tails for me. And I'll handle the gun . . ."

"The gun?" Sundry screamed.

Anthony put in with calm cynicism: "You're taking this a bit far, aren't you?" And spoiled it by giving me one of his special smiles. It would have been devastating on the stage.

"We've got to do the thing right," David persisted. "And Fisher himself has said that the mechanism didn't once fail for him. Perhaps,. if Amaryllis is nervous, he'd like to go inside himself . . ."

"I know what you're doing," Fisher shouted. "You're trying to make a fool of me. But I know! She did it. She's going to pay for it . . ."

Then Sundry's chair crashed over backwards and he was on his feet, his left hand reaching for Fisher's lapels, and George moved so fast that I hadn't seen him get to his feet, and had them separated in a moment.

David spoke as though nothing had happened. "Or perhaps Fisher was lying when he said it'd always worked for him."

"No." Amaryllis spoke from behind me. We had been so immersed in our own scene that we had not noticed her approach along the length of the ballroom. "Martin wasn't lying," she said. "It was working."

"But you said . . ." I couldn't help it, couldn't help turning and rising to my feet, if only to level my eyes with hers. "You said it'd failed the last few times. Amaryllis why were you so frightened? Why," I accused her, "did you leave him alone in the room that night, if you weren't terrified?"

She shrugged. Her eyes were all pitiful contempt for me. She was in her dressing-gown, flamboyantly black with a red dragon design, with beneath it, I saw, her ballet shoes, which was why she had been so silent approaching.

"I had to tell you a lie about the failures or you wouldn't have believed how frightened I was. Konrad said he had to have at least 20 successes with the dummy before I could try it." There was silence. I didn't think she seemed quite sane. "But I knew he intended to kill me that first time he got me in there."

"Why?" asked David. His half-raised hand silenced the rest of us.

"He found it was the only way he could get rid of me," she said negligently, her eyes blank. "Where else could I go, though? But you . . . David . . . you don't want to get rid of me, do you?" He shook his head, not trusting his voice. "Then for you we will re-create it."

Her hair was tied back with a ribbon, her eyes huge with the make-up they use, her head poised on the slender neck. "But that'll be later," she decided. "And now . . ." A glance at Anthony, mocking and challenging. "I think I'm in the mood for Coppélia."

The exit was perhaps the most compelling she had ever made. I saw Abel standing by the far door. What he made of the scene I don't know, but he held the door open for her with a courtly gesture. She walked past him with her flat-footed, toes-out ballet walk.

"Finish your chips, love," said David.

TWELVE

Detective Chief Inspector Abel was both pleased and disappointed with the secret room. He had predicted its existence, and it's always pleasant to have such deductions confirmed. But he had, finally, to reach George's conclusion, which was that Konrad had not been shot there. Yet he was inflexible in this contention that he had certainly not been shot in the laboratory.

"Apart from the impossibility of his murderer having got out of there why would the rug be taken up to the other room, when there was an open window?"

David considered it. The four of us were alone in the Cleric's Library, me basking in the thought that this must mean I was no longer a suspect.

"A body," David decided, "might not turn up, and anything else could conceivably be destroyed by the sea and the rocks. But not a rug. A rug's almost indestructible. It might even get stuck on the rocks and be exposed by the low tide. Yes, I think I'd take it away, if it'd been me."

The difficulty was that nobody could confirm that that specific rug had been in the laboratory at all. There were half a dozen old and stray rugs scattered about its floor. That could have been one of them.

"So we'll keep looking," said Abel.

"For somewhere else? A flat or a cottage?"

Abel smiled his thin smile. "Or even another room he could've been shot in. Another window he could have been dumped from. In the meantime . . ." He produced the gun from his pocket. "I'll take this along."

"Ah!" George pounced in. "So you're admitting it's possible."

"I'm covering my bets."

So at least David was robbed of his most dangerous prop, and there now seemed a possibility that he'd have to call off the demonstration altogether. But somehow I doubted it. After half an hour alone in the lounge with Delibes, Amaryllis had emerged in a state of high ecstasy, half drunk, I thought, with the excess of it after all this time, and she had been wildly in favour of the demonstration; in fact had demanded it. She hung, almost, on David's arm, when he needed no persuasion, and jollied him along with her eyes, and he laughed her off with casual promises. So how was he going to get out of it now?

The answer was that he wasn't. When the place was clear of detectives, and every corner had been scoured for leftovers, he announced that it would be at ten o'clock. It required much hammering on doors to make certain the message—the command—had been conveyed. It required somebody, and it had to be me, to visit Clarice in her room, and not simply persuade her that she had to be there—not too difficult when the sanctity of her insurance claim was mentioned—but also to borrow Konrad's spare white tie, dress shirt and tails.

You see, David was coldly, implacably determined to do it as a complete performance. I could have killed him. In fact, my exasperation finally overcame me.

This happened in our room. It was perhaps 9.30. Outside, the wind blew spray on our windows, part rain, part sea, and inside our lights were flickering. David stood in Konrad's trousers and shirt, the inside leg only one inch too long, the waist only one inch too tight.

"How long is this going on, David?"

"This?" He pulled the waistcoat tight.

"This pretence. You were in her room. All right. You could well have said you were questioning her, in spite of the fact that you've questioned no one else in *their* room. But maybe I'd have accepted it. And then you had to come out with some ridiculous excuse of searching for her outfit."

You will see, I was quite calm about it. I was handling something precious.

"It happened to be the truth," he declared. I perhaps made a derogatory sound. "The first thing that came to me. I didn't have time for a good lie."

"Oh, really, David, and to take it this far! You don't have to lay all this on, just to prove your pitiful little story."

"Sorry. I didn't realise you thought it was pitiful. I

was laying it on in any event."

"That's ridiculous! And now . . . why, you haven't even got the gun. What do you do—say bang?"

"But I've got this."

Then, from the dressing-table drawer, from among *my* underclothes, he produced a little pistol.

My first reaction: "Where did you get that?"

"It's George's. He had it in his car. Not the right model, not even the right calibre, but I don't think anybody'll notice, do you?"

It took my breath away. That he could go into such detail . . . ,

Then the lights gave one more flicker and went out.

"Don't move," he said. "I've got some matches in my other pocket."

"Why should I move?"

"I thought you were about to slap my face. Ah, here we are." I heard the scrape. The flame lit his face weirdly. Then he reached for the lamp and lifted the chimney, and my heart settled when the flame caught. I realised why we all had lamps. Those few moments of darkness, with the wind thudding against the walls, had been terrifying.

The light grew as he replaced the chimney. "David . . ." I began again, hoping desperately that I could still avert the demonstration, "David, I . . ."

Then we heard the screams.

The lamp was still in David's hand, his face illuminated with what seemed sudden triumph. "Come on," he shouted, and he headed for the door.

I forgot I was in slacks and my bra. The screams were high with terror, confined by that inflexible stone. I stumbled through the door and saw George a yard or so behind him. I was being left alone in the darkness, and ran, my bare feet silent, ran towards the light which streamed, rising and falling in yellow and red, from an open doorway along the gallery. I ran, and screamed myself because fire is a primitive evil.

There were shouts now and a slamming of doors. Shadows blundered and David's lamp, the only one, led the confused race for the doorway. I was 20 feet short when Amaryllis fell back from her room, beating at her smouldering dressing-gown, which suddenly flared into naked flame as though the dragon belched it.

David, at a flat run, slid the lamp on to the table which should already have one and didn't. I got there in time to prevent his from sliding off and making things worse, as he dived—a running tackle—at Amaryllis, sending them rolling together in a ball of smoke along the corridor. George pounced on them, slapping hands like shovels on the smoking material, tearing it from her in shreds, until David climbed upright and she lay at their feet, her screams now sobs, with nothing on at all but the black smears of the smouldering scraps.

The room was a furnace. I stumbled into Clarice, who seemed shocked into insensibility on her feet. "Extinguishers," I shouted "Extinguishers, Clarice!"

She shook her head, but Anthony knew. He ran, calling over his shoulder: "This way, this way," and he and George returned to the head of the staircase, where the extinguishers stood—and I'd never noticed—each side the banisters.

David was on his knees again beside Amaryllis. He wasn't wearing a jacket to cover her with. I knelt beside him. He turned to face me, his eyebrows singed. "I think it's mainly shock," he said quietly. "The burns are only minor."

She whimpered. He asked her what had happened.

Gusts of heat moved past us. I didn't think it mattered what had happened, not just then. But David persisted.

"The . . ." she whispered, "the door opened. The lights . . . they'd gone out. I was . . . groping for matches. The door opened . . . there was light. I thought . . . someone being kind . . . kind . . ." She sobbed. "Then he . . . he threw the lamp right at me. I . . . managed to move and it crashed on the floor, and there was one . . . terrible . . ."

She'd have screamed again. I put my hand on her arm. Shudders ran through her. Then I stood up, wondering whether we shouldn't all be heading for the open air.

With my head higher, I found the smoke to be choking me. I bent my head. David was saying: "Who? Did you see who?" But she shook her head. Her protest was almost a howl. "I don't know!"

"We've got to get her away from here, David." But he didn't hear.

I turned. Clarice was screaming now, flapping wildly at Sundry's offered assistance. This time he wasn't going to be rejected. Half carrying her, he struggled away through the smoke.

George and Anthony were inside the room. I peered inside with trepidation. White and black billowing clouds were shot through with scarlet, and flames ran wild up the curtains. George was like a tree-trunk, unmoving in the heat as he played the spray. Anthony was darting here and there, fidgeting at fresh surges of fire. But already it seemed that it was contained. The walls were solid rock, and only the room's contents would burn, and perhaps the floor, and perhaps the ceiling . . .

I felt panic engulfing me. David said: "Watch her,

Elsa. I'm going to look for another."

She was in a tight ball of terror and would not move at my touch. All I could do was crouch beside her. Smoke set me coughing again, and I caught only a glimpse of David running through it, carrying two more extinguishers.

Then there came a time when there was no more than steam eddying from the open door. There was an acrid smell. I ventured to the door. There were no more flames, but the room was a complete wreck. I didn't fancy the thought of telling Amaryllis that all her beautiful clothes were destroyed, and all her personal belongings.

David saw me and came over. The splendid suit of tails was a mess, the shirt black, his face red through the grime.

"It's all right now. Can you get her to our room?"

Which of course was the only possibility, and David had found time to consider it. She would have to share our room with me, David moving in temporarily with George. I thought about it.

"I'll get Clarice," I told him.

"Shake her out of it. Slap her around a bit, if you have to. There'll be some cleaning up to do."

He meant Amaryllis, I thought, though that was before I reached a mirror. But I went straight to Clarice's room, expecting the worst, and therefore was agreeably surprised.

Clarice was the type that always bounces back. Perhaps a lot of her youthful domineering persistence had gone with the years, but it had left behind a stubborn inflexibility. And something Sundry had just said to her, or she to him, had shaken life into her. This was her home, after all. Her eyes went quickly to me.

"How is it?"

It, not she. I told her things were in control, and we'd not need the fire brigade. Her face was smudged, and she recognised it in my eyes, reaching for a mirror.

"My dear, you look terrible," she said, glancing back at me.

"Never mind that. We need a dressing-gown and your biggest pot of cold cream, and you'll have to come and help me with her."

Her eyes went dull. "Stupid creature, she deserves all she gets."

"It was *not* an accident. Now do what I say and get off your behind. Auden, surely you could help with the clearing up. It's chaos in there."

I bustled her. She protested, but I wasn't having any arguments; she was no longer my head prefect. We eventually paraded along the Gallery with our arms loaded with luxurious and therefore comforting clothing, with cleansing cream and soothing lotions, and found Amaryllis sitting with her back to the wall and using language I'm sure they don't encourage at Covent Garden. Unless it's the market. David had just told her the condition of her room.

Clarice and I got her along to my bed. We cleaned her, and discovered the burns to be superficial, painful only when touched with a cream-loaded wad of cotton-wool. Clarice enjoyed this so much that I left her to it and went looking for a bath, if only for David to find me clean and sweet and smelling lovely.

I didn't reach it. David was in the other room, the door open, arguing with George. They were like a couple of scarecrows. George was saying:

"But it doesn't prove anything, Dave. Nothing, damn it."

"We expected something."

"But not this."

They realised I was there. David turned to me. "Elsa love, why don't you go and clean up . . ."

I was about to turn away, but he realised his lack of tact in time, and caught my shoulders in his two filthy hands, and flinched.

"You're hurt," I said quickly.

"No, it's nothing."

"Let me see."

"No, really . . ."

George put in: "Is the heater working? I'll go and have a bath." And he shambled out.

David smelt of smoke and sweat and singed flesh. I took him over to one of the beds and told him to stay there and I'd be back, and rushed in on Clarice and Amaryllis, who were conducting a silent campaign of mutual hatred, then back with the cleansing fluid and cold cream.

"Elsa," he said, "there's something you ought to know."

"Not now."

"Now." There was something special in his voice. I looked up from his puffy, red palms. "I've got to tell you why we were going to have the reconstruction."

"It'll do later."

"It *is* later. Later than I should have told you. So it's now. It was the gun, you see. It'd jammed when the murderer tried to fire a second shot."

"But I thought you said the first shot went through the cabinet panel and into the dummy, David."

"Whatever it did," he said impatiently, "it refused to do it a second time. And as Konrad had a gunshot wound in his chest, I'm working on the assumption that *he* didn't fire the first."

"Keep your hands still."

"So—on an assumption, then—that the murderer knows the gun jammed, and nobody else does, I thought if we set it up, and got Amaryllis in the cabinet, and fancied it all up with the right clothes and a bit of blah, it might seem real enough for everybody to expect I'd really fire the gun. And then . . . whoever protested wouldn't know the gun had jammed. Whoever didn't would be the one who'd used it."

I kept my eyes down. My heart was bounding. "But why didn't you tell me before?"

"I was ashamed." His voice was low. I lifted my eyes. His mouth was miserable.

"Of what?" I whispered.

"Of the idea. It was cheap and paltry and inconclusive." And my heart plummetted.

Still reaching for it: "There're worse things to be ashamed of."

"Not in my book. I like to prove things, argue them through. To tell you the truth, I'm glad it's off. What if *nobody* had stopped me?"

"But, David!" I couldn't stand his distress. "Somebody *did* intervene."

"Yes," he agreed desperately. "We were arguing about that, George and me. Somebody went to pretty drastic lengths to stop it coming off. But I'd argued that only a non-murderer would intervene—in ignorance that the gun had jammed—so are we going to assume that the intervention, which was a near-fatal incident, was just to prevent a possibly fatal one? That's taking it a bit far. And if it was the murderer who threw that lamp, why should he do it unless he'd seen through my bluff, in which event it wouldn't need such drastic action just to double-bluff me. I mean, he'd only got to raise his voice at the reconstruction and pretend he thought the gun would work."

"Oh dear, David, you are getting yourself tied up." My mind wasn't on it. The sympathy didn't exactly flood over him. "Does everything have to be logical for you? People don't react in logical ways, not all the time."

"And they don't go to great lengths just to make puzzles for mugs like me. They do what they've got to do, when there's no alternative."

"You're getting a bit pompous, David. Don't condescend to me, please."

He looked at his hands. "And you, my love, are not being very logical, covering my hands with cream when I've still got to take a bath."

He was holding them away from him, as though mortally offended. I couldn't help laughing at his twitching nose. "Oh, David, why didn't you tell me? You knew what I was thinking."

"That was ridiculous."

"Not worth consideration?"

"I've just said it was ridiculous." Then at last he smiled, and how could I mistrust that stupid, blackened and hurt face?

So that after all the cold cream wasn't wasted, most of it finishing on my bare skin, which, I realised when George returned, was still mainly uncovered. Still more uncovered, rather.

He was wearing David's dressing-gown, so must have been in next door for it.

"How is she?" I asked. I did what I could with my hair.

"Aftermath," he said. "Exhausted."

"Is Clarice staying with her?" I asked hopefully, wondering where David and I might discover a bed we could share. And David echoed my own mournful thought.

"You can't imagine that, surely!"

"Then *I'll* have to."

"I'd realised that."

"Then you might have shown some consideration and kept your hands to yourself. George," I said, "keep an eye on him. He's suffering from too many fancy ideas."

George grinned. "So I see. But *I* can't stay with her."

"Good heavens, no."

They laughed. I suppose I'd been a bit coy, but I was bouncing with happiness and willing to go along with it. I even paused at the door, vaguely aware that I must have looked a sight. But two pairs of eyes encouraged me to believe it wasn't unpleasant.

"Get some sleep," I said.

Then I went to do my duties as night nurse.

THIRTEEN

I am not denying that I got a little sleep. But George had been wrong about the exhaustion. Amaryllis might have been maudlin, even a little delirious, but she was not tired. So I went from David's arms to her mumbled, tearful torrent of self-pity, and if hers was worse than mine I was sorry for her.

Most of the night was taken up by a recital of her passionate, and rather sordid affair with Konrad, and I had never realised that anyone could be so inflamed by desire as to be completely helpless, and at the same time miserable with longing for what she had left behind. Oh, make no mistake, it was a past dream now. With ballet, there's no let-up. You can never recapture that certain edge . . . To my fury I was beginning to feel for her, actually sympathise . . .

I slept. I awoke to her voice, wailing that he was gone, gone . . . I tried her with brandy and she seemed to relax, the tears still hot on her cheeks. I slept again.

". . . not really ballet," she was saying, "but close enough, so I could fool myself that I hadn't deserted it. But when the act folded . . ."

I think I dozed. The tap on the door woke me. It was David.

"Aren't you coming down to breakfast, love?"

Somewhere in the confusion my own bath had been forgotten. I was lying on the top of the bed, still in the same slacks. Amaryllis slept like a conscienceless child, and David looked fresh and vibrant.

"When I've had a bath," I said.

"I had to shave in cold water. The heater's not working."

What I needed was a small allowance of sympathy myself. He said he'd see me downstairs, then, and did I know where George could find a length of rope, and, when I did get down there, not to worry because he'd remembered the tow-rope in the back of his car. Then he went to help George measure it, or something.

I think David must have done the cooking, because it was his touch with the bacon. I discovered I was ravenously hungry; that it was raining, from Fisher, who had been for a walk and claimed he hadn't heard a word the previous night; that Clarice would be down, from Sundry, who might not have left her side all night; and that Amaryllis was having a fit, from Anthony, who had been in her room examining the mess when she'd walked in.

Anthony, it seemed, had been there all night, just to

see that nothing smouldering should burst into flames. It was his home too.

"Blames me for it," he said morosely. "What she needs is a good spanking."

And she might, I thought, even enjoy it.

Then George came in and said there I was and was I ready.

"Didn't Dave tell you," he asked. "We need you for a small experiment."

"Why me?" I demanded. "Why must it always be me?"

"You're the lightest, Elsa."

I was about to suggest Amaryllis, but then decided he included her, and how could I resist such a sweet compliment?

"I hope you're not taking me up to that room again, George."

"Well, as a matter of fact, yes."

"No wonder I'm light, you're wearing me out."

"More theories?" Anthony inquired, returning to his old sarcasm.

"Trying out an idea," agreed George affably.

Fisher's head came up. "Oh, nobody can beat you for trying. If it's ideas you want—"

"Thank you, no."

"And if you," said Sundry, moving aggressively towards Fisher, "make one more accusation against Clarice, I'll pile so many lawyers on you that you'll die of suffocation."

"Threats, threats!"

"Oh, Lord," said George, "let's get out of here."

David was waiting in the hall, looking restless. Whatever George's idea might have been, it was clear that David did not share it. He was worried, and shot brief and anxious glances at me. I noticed that he was holding his hands clear of his sides.

"Let me see them."

"Elsa, please . . . Listen to what George has got to say."

George beamed, but didn't get round to saying it because it was then that we heard the car on the gravel outside. David and George looked at each other, and I went to open the door.

It was Abel and his sergeant.

Seeing the three of us together he plunged straight in with what he had to say, his voice amiable enough but his eyes cold.

"I hear you've had some trouble in the night. I *hear* it. I was not informed. Nobody called the police, and yet I understand there was an attempt on Miss Moore's life."

"We'd better go somewhere," said David.

"I think we should."

As I followed them I realised it must have seemed strange that nobody had phoned the police. But really, only David, George and myself knew that the fire had been started deliberately, apart from my one casual remark to Clarice, which had gone over her head.

We found the Cleric's Library to be empty. Abel seemed disinclined to sit, but the rest of us did.

"How did you hear?" From David.

"An anonymous phone-call."

"Ha!" From George.

Only the three of us knew—and Amaryllis.

"What does that mean?" asked Abel.

George shrugged. "It was not necessarily an attempt on her life. She's highly strung, and loves a bit of self-dramatisation. Else why should she phone you?"

"And fail to give her name," Abel pointed out. "Where's the dramatisation there? Somebody'd better tell me all about it."

David took it up. In one corner of the room, unobtrusively, the sergeant was scribbling in his notebook. It was a comfort to realise that at least we three were now trusted.

Or so I thought at that time.

David concluded his statement. He does that sort of thing very well.

"I should have left a couple of men here," Abel muttered in self-criticism.

"You weren't to know . . ."

But Abel's glance at David was angry; he did not welcome comfort from anyone but a superior. But David met his eyes steadily, and his voice was quiet when he went on: "None of us expected anything like that, though I at least should have expected something."

"Why?" It positively cracked.

David looked at me, I thought with apology. "I was trying to rig a scene to trap the murderer."

"You had no right!"

"Based on the fact that an attempt was made to fire two shots from that gun, but it jammed on the second. Only the murderer could know that, and I thought—"

"You thought! *You* did? I'm the one to do the thinking around here. I've a good mind to hold you for impeding the course . . ."

"What damned course?" said George flatly. "We couldn't see anything going on."

Abel seemed more pale and more tense with the growth of his anger. "And you're two ex-policemen! It's clear why they chucked you out! You know as well as I do that it's routine that counts, the sifting, the detail—"

"And the failing to notice," David observed, "that

the gun had jammed."

"I am aware of that."

"Now, yes. And made what out of it?"

"I'm not here to answer your questions. And the blasted gun's got nothing to do with it."

"No?"

And then Abel was abruptly calm. It was as though he had realised he was not getting anywhere, and was losing control of the interview. "I think not," he said. "I think not indeed. You're sidetracking the real issue. We know the gun was fired once. There is one bullet hole in the cabinet, and there was a crash heard when the cabinet fell over, or was pushed, or whatever. That much we must accept. But because there's one bullet hole in Konrad Klein's body, and one shot was fired, you're letting it confuse you. You've got to go for essentials."

"Such as?" asked George with interest.

Then at last Abel did take a seat, though only on the arm of an easy chair, his manner casual. He might have been lecturing at the Police Academy.

"The fact that *somebody* walked out of that room. Either Klein did so himself, and was therefore alive when he did it, or he was shot in there, his body dumped out of the window, and his murderer walked out. *That* is the basic, essential fact.

David said: "Unarguable. Or is it? There could be ways."

"Which I've examined in detail. D'you think my men have been standing around, doing nothing but eat chips! There was apparently no place of concealment in the room, if we're to accept what Anthony Klein said as truth."

"But . . ." I began, but he gestured, and I was silent.

"And that leaves the window," he said. "You've all seen it. Out of there, either up or down, is impossible without a rope. There's no evidence that any rope was ever inside the room, so it would need to have been taken there. By the murderer or by Klein himself. But to do what? It could not have been fastened, earlier, to the roof, because the trapdoor hadn't been opened in a score of years. It could not have been tossed up over one of the crenellations around the edge, not with any chance of success—and we're talking about something planned. It could have been used to slide downwards perhaps, but to where? There *are* windows beneath that one—though none above—but those, too, are about fixed solid, and there's no evidence of one being opened. Can we agree that the window could not have been used?"

David and George agreed. They nodded to each other. Abel took it that they were exchanging complimentary gestures, and went on with enthusiasm.

"And so, that's the whole point. Somebody got out of that door, cabinet or not. The question is, how? Get the how and we get the somebody. There's already been some talk about how the cabinet got there. Well, that's not the point, unless the way it got there explains how somebody managed to get out. Oh, I know we've had one demonstration of that, but we're a bit short of men as strong as Coe here—unless Klein himself could have done it. But we all know that when Coe tried it there were score marks down the door, which weren't there before. So . . . any other suggestions?"

Again the impression of a training session; a problem in logic. But I was suspicious of this previously angry man now calmly asking for advice. George grunted, though, as though to speak, then shook his head. But David said: "That means you've got an idea."

"Something. An idea—or the only possibility left. That's why I came here, to speak to your wife."

Then slowly, and I found terrifyingly, he turned to face me.

"I wanted to take you through a few points again."

"Yes," I whispered. I glanced at David, who was leaning forward in his chair. He nodded encouragingly. I cleared my throat. "Very well."

"You said you heard the shot and the crash?"

"Yes."

"Because your window was open?"

"That's right."

"But you said it was a cold night."

I swallowed. His eyes seemed to take me apart. "The wind was from the sea, and my window faces the courtyard. It was . . . fresh."

"If your window faces the courtyard, and *his* faces the sea, how could you have heard anything?"

I considered that. "The wind carried the sound—it echoed perhaps in the courtyard. But I did hear it."

"But your friend Clarice only heard the crash."

"She didn't say . . ."

"She said it to me."

"I'm sorry. I thought it was a question."

"No need to apologise," he said with annoying condescension. "You both heard it, and you both ran for the Tower."

"Yes."

"She leading?"

"Well . . . yes. If it matters."

"I'll decide that. You reached the door to the room. It wouldn't open. Who turned the ring of the latch?"

"I think . . . yes, she did."

"You didn't try it yourself?"
"Well, no."
"Why not?"
"Why should I?"
"It'd perhaps be natural. The attitude: here, let me have a go."
"I didn't try it."
"So, for all you know, she may not have turned the handle enough to release the latch inside?"
"But why . . . I mean, she wouldn't *do* such a thing." I looked towards David for assistance, and he sat like stone, his lips tight, his eyes on Abel. He inclined his head a fraction. "It'd be natural for her to turn it all the way," I said firmly.
"Or you thought she did."
"I have no reason to doubt it." I could be as formal as him.
"Very well. We'll leave that. You turned and went down to fetch one of the men, and met Anthony Klein coming up. Is that so?"
"Yes."
"You mentioned he was not out of breath."
"He was coming up slowly. I merely meant . . . he's a fit man."
"Or he had not come far."
"I don't understand."
"I think you do."
"No . . . no . . ."
"You're not stupid. If he'd not come far, where could he have been?"
"You're saying it, not me. *You* say what you mean."
"That attitude doesn't help. Where . . . could . . . he . . . have . . . been?"
Then George grunted and I heard him move. At last Dave spoke. "No, George." I fought for what Abel

wanted, angry that he'd provoked me to it.

"In the room below?" I offered.

"But I've said the rooms hadn't been opened."

"You said the windows," I said angrily.

"That's what I like, an eye for detail. You're quite correct—but the doors too. So, with your powers of observation . . . what else about the doors?"

"Oh . . . I don't know. I just don't . . ."

"They're deeply set. At least a foot."

"You're not saying . . ." I was aware that my voice was breaking.

"What?" he asked quietly.

"That Anthony . . . stood in a doorway . . . and we *passed* him going up!"

"Why not? A slim man in a dark suit—it *was*, you know, I asked him—with his face and hands covered . . ."

"You're just being stupid."

"I'm sorry that you said that. I was going to suggest that your friend, leading, carrying the lamp—is *that* correct?"

"Yes, she was carrying it."

"Then she'd be dazzled, and the lamp would throw the shadow of the door recess forward for her, hiding him. But for you? Perhaps. But you say I'm stupid. So maybe I'm wrong that you missed him. Maybe you *saw* him there . . ."

"By Christ!" George burst out, and David said flatly: "Don't bully my wife, friend, with your inverted logic."

Abel never glanced away from me.

"Of course I didn't see him!" I cried.

His mouth flexed. He was amused at my lies. "Very well. Take it on. Anthony went back up with you. *He* turned the ring handle and put his shoulder to the door. And it moved slowly. But he comes of a family of illusionists. What if the door did *not* have the cabinet behind it, and he was simply giving an impression of effort . . ."

I was very tired and my head swam. "I heard the cabinet move," I said impatiently.

"But did you? You *expected* to hear something move, and . . ."

"I *heard* it."

"But he could have groaned with effort."

"It was a sliding sound."

"Which he imitated with his mouth."

"All I know is that it sounded like something sliding."

"Ah, that's better."

"It's not better or worse," I shouted. "It's just fact."

"Quite so. But you're also saying that the room was empty. You saw it searched by Anthony."

"It was empty."

"No one hiding—not even behind the door?"

"I don't know what you mean," I said wearily.

"Anthony said the wind almost took the door from his hand. So he was holding it open, was he?"

"I suppose so."

"Suppose? Don't you know?"

"I had my back to him. I went to shut the window."

"But when you turned back?"

"It was . . . open. But that's just plain . . . ridiculous."

A tiny smile reached his eyes that I'd flinched from the word stupid. "Isn't it?" he asked. "So all we're left with—the *only* possibility is that the cabinet was not against the door."

"But I heard it sliding back!" I moaned.

"An imaginative woman, impressionable."

"You've gone far enough," David suddenly broke in,

his voice harsh. "All you've come up with is a theory involving Anthony. So go and arrest him—but leave my wife alone."

"Do you think I've got a case?" Abel turned to him in interest, not at all affected by David's tense anger. "I didn't take you to be slow-witted. Now—what have I been saying?" He paused, luring David to a defence of his own intelligence. But David remained silent. Abel's voice became more brittle.

"I'm saying that he could not have done it alone. I know he's a professional conjuror. I've taken that into account. I've wondered if he could have fixed that door latch so that only he could turn it fully. But even allowing that as a possibility he would still not have had time, between the crash of the cabinet and the expected arrival of *somebody*, to get right down the Tower stairs and on to the Gallery, without being seen. And so—he would need somebody as an accomplice, to mount those stairs and not see him hidden in a doorway below. Deliberately not see him. And thus give him an alibi of a sort, if he found he needed one. But who? That's the point. There's been talk of complicity to defraud. This is more serious—complicity to murder. So I have to ask myself: did he fix it with his stepmother, she to pretend to turn the latch—and your wife arrived unexpectedly on the scene, and failed to spot him hiding? Or did he fix it with your wife—the stepmother being the one to miss him—and your wife being the one to try the latch—and be lying about it? Or did he work it with both? You can see my difficulty."

George choked out something quite obscene, and David thumped him on the shoulder just in time to restrain him. Then David got to his feet and flexed his shoulders.

"You making a charge?"
"Not at the moment."
"Not even that she's so stupid that she failed to see a man in a doorway?"
"She might," conceded Abel, "have been looking down at her feet."
"I notice that you didn't suggest that earlier," said David, and he sounded very dangerous to me.
"You know the methods of interrogation . . ."
"I suggest you go and try it on somebody else. Now. You and your sergeant. Eh?"
And Abel stared at him for one moment before turning on his heel and heading for the door. His sergeant followed him. The door closed behind them.
"I'll kill him!" said George.
"It wouldn't help," David replied, and then I was weeping in his arms, and truly, in that moment, I could have killed him too.

FOURTEEN

Everything seemed to be coming from a long way away. I was aware that I was comfortable in a large, soft chair, too comfortable to remain awake, really. Two serious, concentrated faces were poised infront of me.

"Now, Elsa, please think," David was saying. "That door latch—are you absolutely certain you didn't touch the ring? Absolutely!"

My own voice, distant and apart: "Yes, there's hardly room for two . . ."

"And Anthony—"

"You're taking it seriously!" I was fighting to bring my conscious mind to the fore. "You're not really—"

"*He's* taking it seriously. It's how he's tackling this. He throws wild theories at people—he'll do it with every one of you—hoping somebody will blurt out an admission. Now think."

"I've got nothing to admit."

George said, his voice rumbling: "It's fantasy to suggest he hid in a doorway."

Now everything was clear, too clear. I could see every worried wrinkle round George's mouth, read the angry, baffled expression in his eyes. "But, George," I said, "a similar thing happened on the battlements. Clarice passed me, a foot away, and it was not even dark. And she didn't see me."

David was impatient. "She was under stress."

"So was I!"

"She had realised it was possible that Sundry had killed Konrad, just to make sure she didn't cheat on their contract and join Konrad after all . . ."

"Oh, dear Lord!" My head swam. I fought for control. "But it's possible I could have missed Anthony in the same way."

"You'd pass him with barely a couple of inches' room."

I sighed. "But possible."

"It's what Abel wants, Elsa. To get you believing the possibility. Then you'd perhaps find yourself distorting your memory, simply for peace of mind."

Didn't David know me? What more was I expected to face, with no chance of turning away?

"But, David, there's one thing nobody can distort. I've got a clear memory of the sound when Anthony pushed open that door. And I've heard it again since." I paused, putting the memories together. Neither spoke. This had to be mine, unforced and unprompted. "When George tried that fantastic experiment with the cabinet perched on the door—then. I heard you dragging the cabinet away. It was a wonderful sound—I couldn't forget it. And the sound made when Anthony opened the door was the same. That I *know*. And nobody's going to distort it for me."

George sighed. David whispered: "That's my girl." And George said: "I'll stick it down his throat."

"No," said David. "We wait. He'll be all day trying various wild ideas on people. We'll see what it brings."

That waiting was terrible. George left us and prowled the battlements. David played Sibelius in the Pink Lounge all morning. I'd have welcomed something less ominous. In the afternoon, David and I went riding, he on the grey and me on the bay mare. The saddlery was old and worn, and I couldn't get the girth tight enough.

We returned early and found that the car had gone. There was tea and sandwiches in the lounge and the atmosphere had the tension of a violin string, tingling the air. But at last it all came out: Abel had tried the same theory on all of us! Nobody would meet my eyes, and I wondered who might have betrayed me, in sheer self-protection.

George got to his feet, crumbs clinging to his shirt and tie. "Well, that's it, Dave."

David looked round. He was still feeling out the reactions. "It only works, what Abel's done, when it's close enough to be the truth. It's only then that a guilty person feels themselves trapped."

It was received in stony silence.

"Coming, Elsa?"

But to where? "Yes, if you like." Then, like a funeral procession, the three of us climbed again to the Tower.

George produced his length of rope. His voice was deep. The rope was 30 feet of blue twisted nylon, half an inch thick. He swirled it as he spoke.

"Abel's about cleared all the possibilities, but he missed one little point. Nowhere anybody could hide in here, he said. Well . . . I did suggest one place, though not too seriously at the time." He glanced up at the joists. "But it's about all we've got left." David grunted and turned away.

With the lights now on, the joists were barely visible. George had three tries before the rope fell over. He handed both ends to me. "So put your weight on it, Elsa. Let's see if that joist'll take even your weight."

"This is ridiculous."

"Try it, please, for me."

"Let's get it over with," said David.

With uncertainty I gripped the rope and bent my legs to bring the weight on my arms. At once I felt it going, and put my feet down again quickly. It creaked up above and flakes of rotten wood fell into my hair.

"Satisfied?" said George.

"Nobody's arguing." David was losing his patience. "But you've only got back to the fact that somebody must have got out, and managed to leave that cabinet against the door. Then how?"

"I'm going to show you how."

Sundry spoke from the door, his head round it. "Are we missing something?" He and Fisher had given way to curiosity. They pushed their way in.

"Ah, Fisher!" said George. "It was you who showed us how the cabinet shot against the door when it operated."

"When it was tilted," said Fisher suspiciously.

David sighed. "And *that* left the murderer on the inside."

"But not," claimed George, "if he could do it from outside."

David groaned. I heard myself give a shaky laugh. We'd already seen one of George's demonstrations.

"I hope this doesn't take too much strength," I said, trying to make a joke of it because George was only groping for ideas, for me.

"Only enough to push over the cabinet and lift a pencil. And it's on castors . . . you see, it could be pushed up to the door with its own door wide open . . . like this." George did it with one hand. The castors rumbled over the naked boards. "And," he went on, "with it there, it was pushed over backwards. Mind yourself." He tilted it gently, and then it went with a rush. I flinched before it struck, and clouds of dust rose with the crash.

He was quite proud of it. The door to the cabinet was wide open still, and I could see he'd been prepared for this because he had one of the dummies in it, an unclothed one. The suit he'd discarded when searching for the missing bullet was lying in the far corner.

"It's primed," George said, "and we all know that it operates as soon as its door closes. Now, you understand, that was the crash you heard. People were used to shots, but not to crashes. From that moment he'd have around two minutes."

"Now wait!" Fisher cried angrily. "You just hold it right there. I can see what you're up to. You've already eliminated Clarice . . ."

"So I have." George beamed at him. "But not you, sir, who came in later from the courtyard. I'll get around to that later."

"I'm not staying to hear this."

"Please yourself. In either event, let's not hear from you again. All right?"

Fisher subsided into sulks. George flexed his shoulders.

"I was saying . . . what he'd do would be to use the end of a pencil to hold open the cabinet door."

He hooked the pencil under the very edge of the cabinet door, which it now left open about a quarter of an inch. It protruded in the direction of the opening edge of the room's door. The castors were a foot and a half from the door. George opened it against the castors. "Made a mistake here," he admitted. "I'll never get through that gap. Slide it back a bit, Dave."

David, unconvinced, lifted the top end of the cabinet and slid it back a foot or so. George just managed to make it.

"Shove it back where it was, Dave."

David did so, and we all squeezed back on to the tiny landing with George. I eyed the protruding pencil a bit warily as I edged past it. It was much like the trigger of a cocked pistol.

We were very short of room out there. Fisher and Sundry had to move up a step or two. George crouched before the partly open door, and George, crouching, left very little of the view showing. But what I could see, peering over his shoulder, was that it was not going to work.

David said: "Oh Lord, here we go again."

The difficulty was that the cabinet had to be behind the door and therefore not quite in sight through the gap, and George was required to reach in with his right hand round the corner, and fumble around.

"Got it," he said. "Now what I reckon is that it'll operate as soon as I jerk out the pencil, and it'll shoot the dummy out . . ." He turned back his head, his voice complacent. ". . . just where it was found, under the window. The trouble is . . ." There came a hint of worry into his voice. "The point is, I reckon the cabinet'll shoot back against the door—"

The pencil came free. No doubt the dummy was shot out. Certainly the cabinet moved back. It did so, smartly, like a recoiling howitzer, and effectively, as George had claimed, slammed the door. The one snag was that George was unable to withdraw his hand quickly enough. The door clamped on it, just below the fingers, and obviously with some force because he let out a bellow of anger and pain.

David shouted: "Shove it open with your shoulder."

But George was fixed in his awkward crouch and had no purchase. He bellowed again. "Get it open!"

"If you'll move over a bit," said David, "I'll get my shoulder to it."

"How the hell can I move over? For God's sake, hurry."

George's body, in one ungainly and condensed bulk, occupied most of the small landing. David could barely find footing behind him, and then he was so crushed against the outside wall, and had to lean so far forward to reach over and beyond George, that he could barely reach the door, let alone put any pressure on it.

"Hurry David," I said, because I was very close to George's anguish.

"I can't get at it, you big oaf," David shouted.

"Then find a flaming axe or something. Smash the thing down." George moaned. I felt hot with distress. For George to express any reaction to pain meant the suffering was extreme.

"Do something, David," I said.

And Anthony came clattering up the stairs, the two women panting behind him.

"An axe?" he said, taking it all in inside a second. "I'll get one," and promptly turned to gallop down again and became horribly entangled with Clarice and

Amaryllis, who screamed at him in their ignorance.

"An axe is no good," said David hollowly. "George, you've got to shift over."

A silence. George's breathing was heavy. Then at last he spoke quietly. "I can't shift at all. I think my hand's broken."

I looked at David. He was very pale. "We'd never smash that door in," he said softly. "Elsa, what did you do with the rope?"

"I . . . I dropped it. What do you mean?"

George gasped: "Do something, Dave."

"Where did you drop it? Look through the gap love. From where you are—can you see it?"

I had one foot on the landing, one on the step below. By leaning forward, David reaching past George with one hand to my shoulder, I could just see the end.

"I see it."

"Where? How far?"

"A foot or two inside."

David's eyes met mine. "Can you reach it?"

I didn't reply. I didn't want to get the rope for him; I didn't want to leave George to suffer. I was caught. I took another step down. There was a gap between George's chest and the hard stone of the landing, a foot gap. I edged my head in and then my shoulders, twisting as I went. George was hot against me. I was now very close to his sweating face. He gave me a ghastly grin. "Good girl." It was a sickly whisper.

The gap between the door and the jamb was the width of the fat part of George's hand, now a little compressed. I slid my own hand through easily enough, against the floor. The wrist was more difficult.

"Now, George," I said, "don't you dare let that door go."

Sweat dripped on my neck. I reached. Now I couldn't see the rope for my own sweat-blinded eyes. Not see it, but feel it, the tips of my fingers brushing it. I forced my arm in farther. The door and the jamb were agony as they scored my forearm. Then I had it. I slowly withdrew my arm. I had it, and nearly wept with the triumph because I knew what David intended.

I crouched, free of George, and gave David the end. He wound it in quickly, and turned to climb the stairs, Sundry and Fisher scrambling out of the way. I could barely get to my feet.

"Don't leave me, David."

He paused and looked back. He knew I could not remain there, and wait. "Come on, then," and he left me to stagger after him. One last groan followed us.

"You first," he said, waiting on the top landing. He had already reached up and torn the trapdoor free. The opening was a bare foot above his head. He caught my waist, and with one easy movement he threw me up, and I crouched as he handed me the rope and elbowed himself up beside me.

"A loop. Quickly." He did it himself. I was aware that it was raining, that the sea pounded, reaching, far below, and that nothing I could say would stop him. In fact, that I could not find it in myself to want to stop him.

"You can do nothing, Elsa. You understand? Nothing. Don't even look down."

There were, indeed, as Abel had said, buttresses which would take a loop of rope. Dave tossed it over, and briefly leaned his weight behind it. Then he threw the end over into the space below, looked at its lie for one second, then was over the edge.

How could he say I must not watch him? I was on my knees, hands on the precious, vibrating rope, and ventured my head beyond it. Below me, the wind swinging him, I thought, helplessly, he was slowly lowering himself. He had a twist of rope round his left leg, resting over his instep, where his right foot trapped it. And below, far below, beyond even the tapering fall of the tower, was the slick, sea-lashed wall of black cliff, and below that the toothed rocks over which the sea pounded.

He was opposite the window. I realised that, because he stopped. And then he was helpless, because the window was set a clear 18 inches into the rock, and he could not hope to reach it, and could not hope to open it if he did. But, to my horror, he put his foot against the wall and thrust himself away, so that on the return of his swing, horribly jerked to a halt by the rope against the wall above, he put his foot through the window.

I heard the crash of glass. He did that three times, and I waited for the final one.

He thrust himself farther away from the wall, and on the backlash of the return he flung himself forward, releasing the rope, and still there was a crash and tinkling of glass as he went through the residue.

"David!"

I ran back to the trapdoor, and realised that I was faced by a sheer drop of seven feet. And no way . . . But you can, you know, you can jump forward in terror and survive with no more than a cut knee and a sharp pain in one ankle, and even hobble down to the landing.

"Get on with it, Dave," George choked, and I heard the familiar dragging of the cabinet. George collapsed on his face, then David threw the door open. He was cut and dirty and dishevelled, and I flung myself at him. Then stopped.

He did not see me. For one moment I thought he was hurt, but then he found me a painful smile, kissed me quickly, and said:

"Come in, all of you. I've got something to tell you."

His palms, I saw, were torn and bleeding.

FIFTEEN

We got George on to the only chair, where he sat with his head bent, his right hand cradled in his left on his lap. The wind was driving wetly through the smashed window.

"Somebody shut the door," said David quietly.

Anthony offered: "I'll phone for an ambulance."

Then George raised his head, his face ghastly. "No. I'm all right."

For a moment his eyes rested on the window opening and he glanced at David, but he said nothing. Seeming to apologise for the drama of it David explained:

"We'd never have shifted that door. The architrave round the top of the cabinet had got itself into a crack between the floorboards."

I saw what he meant. Some of the gaps were a good half an inch, the boards running parallel to the door.

"If that's the case . . ." George drew in a breath, grimacing. ". . . why didn't it stick on that night, when Anthony shoved it open?"

"That's what I was thinking." David's eyes were bright, almost feverish. He seemed to ignore the rest of us, speaking only to George. "It must have been at an angle. I mean, the bottom of the cabinet couldn't have been flat against the door, so it wasn't pointing straight at the window. And if that was the case, it wasn't going to throw the dummy where it was found, under the window. It'd be more like six feet to one side or the other, I reckon. And we know that *something* was thrown out, because the mechanism had worked—it was in a worked position. Also we know that it wasn't Konrad who was thrown out, because he wasn't shot inside the cabinet, and something was. Makes you think, don't it?"

George shook his head shaggily. "I don't seem to be thinking straight. Seems to me you've got a contradiction there, Dave."

"I really think I ought to phone for a doctor, at least," said Anthony.

Amaryllis stirred. She was wearing, I saw, my pale blue slacks and my best white lace blouse. She seemed shocked by David's exploit. "No . . . I'll go."

"Not for me." And George was rigid against a spasm of pain. "Wait'n hear what Dave's got to say."

"I'll keep it short," said David. "A contradiction, yes. I'm saying that the dummy was ejected, but everybody knows that if it was, in Konrad's illusion, the bullet would've missed it, and ploughed through both sides of the cabinet. That fits with the dummy not having a bullet in it, but as the bullet *didn't* go through both sides, then it must have gone into the dummy. Did somebody say something?"

I'd heard it too, a moan, and it hadn't been George. I looked round. There was a poise to all of them; no one stood near any of the others. All eyes were on David. He shrugged.

"No matter. I'm sure somebody was going to point out that Konrad could've thrown the dummy over there beneath the window, if the thing had failed. But could he? Look at it like this. One shot was fired—there was one crash as the cabinet fell over. Abel put it quite simply: somebody, either Konrad or his murderer, left the room after the cabinet fell. But we've exhausted all chances of Konrad having left this room and having been shot elsewhere. One gun, one shot, and I think everybody's quite convinced that Konrad died with that shot. So it follows that he didn't get round to throwing the dummy under the window."

David looked round as though assessing the possibility. Fisher was proclaiming his uninterest by reaching through the window for the rope, tugging it tentatively.

"Hurry it up, Dave, huh?" George murmured.

"Sorry, George. Where was I? Yes. Konrad being shot in here. But there was only one shot, and that shot must have done three things: put a hole in the cabinet, lodged in the dummy, and killed Konrad."

"But, Dave . . . there wasn't any bullet in the dummy."

David dragged his hands down his face. It left it smeared with blood, but he grinned. "Gets worse, doesn't it! We've got a bullet that had to go into the dummy, because there was nowhere else for it to go, and we've got a dummy with no bullet in it thrown across the room to a position it wouldn't have landed. And we've got the fact that the cabinet couldn't have operated anyway if the dummy was still there to receive the bullet."

"I've had enough of this," said Fisher, and he headed for the door.

"Please stay where you are."

I saw that David held George's gun. To all intents and purposes it was the murder weapon—but the murderer had to know it could not fire. David and his petty tests? Surely not—he'd denigrated the subterfuge. But Fisher jerked to a halt. His head came up.

"That's a criminal offence, using a weapon to restrain somebody."

"I asked you . . . please."

Fisher shrugged. "But it's cold in here." And Anthony laughed derisively. "Try stopping me!" he said, and moved casually.

The bullet slammed the door its last two inches.

"This is *not* the same gun," said David calmly. "I'm only asking you to listen. All right?"

A gust of wind swirled rain through the window. They withdrew, I felt, more from the chill than from the gun.

"What we're rather forgetting," said David, "is that the mechanism in that cabinet operates when the door shuts. We've been rather brain-washed into the idea that the shot always had to come immediately after the door was shut. But it isn't so. The shot doesn't have to be related to the door at all. In fact, the door could have been shut after the shot, for once. *Then* the dummy could have been ejected with the bullet already in it. So, take that as a basic, and examine all the alternatives of sequence, and you have to come to one conclusion. The bullet must have penetrated

Konrad's chest first, right through him, then had sufficient force left to go on through the cabinet panel, and then lodged in the dummy. It's the only thing. And if, after that, the cabinet door was shut, then the dummy, complete with bullet, would be thrown out. Of course, we've still got to explain why the cabinet crashed to the floor and then recoiled against the door. Well, what is more sensible to visualise than Konrad standing beside the cabinet when he was shot, the dummy inside and the cabinet door open, and when he fell or staggered, himself pushing the cabinet over backwards. So that was when the door shut and the mechanism worked."

I saw that George was no longer able to make objections. I couldn't do anything for him, but I could say what he would have said.

"But it leaves two of your queries unsettled, David. There wasn't a bullet in the dummy and, according to you, it would've landed a few feet to one side of the window."

"That," he admitted, "is the big snag. But you see what it means: the dummy ejected and the dummy we found were not the same one. They'd been exchanged. And I didn't really realise I could prove that until I got into here in such an unconventional way."

"Well!" Sundry stepped forward. He looked round for approval, and I realised how pompous he could be. "I think I'm speaking for all of us in this. If that's all you've got to tell us I'd rather leave it until we get downstairs."

"It's not all," David claimed easily. "Not if you think what it means. There was a shot and a crash and within two or three minutes there could be expected a rush of company. The gun had been picked up from the table, there was a simple and straightforward firing of it—and an attempted second shot, incidentally—and then . . . what? The cabinet was blocking the door, and time was running out with certain discovery—and what is done about it? The dummies are switched, that's what. The blood-stained rug is rolled up, to hide the *fact* of murder, and probably hidden behind the dummy against the wall, and in the next two minutes one dummy is switched for the other. Imagine what that means in practice. The dummy was dressed in its outfit of tights, tails and a flat sort of top hat. All those would have to be switched over—in two minutes!—and the dummy chosen to receive them happened to be one with no bullet in it."

They were staring at him as though he had gone mad.

"And the whole thing spoiled by leaving the new one beneath the window instead of a few feet to one side," David added.

"Well . . . this is the craziest—" began Clarice. But Anthony cut her short savagely. "Let him say it!"

"Anthony's seen what I'm getting at," David said with approval. "I think he's known for some time. Why else did we get *Coppélia*?"

Clarice screamed at that point and caught at Amaryllis's arm.

David smiled. "But of course, you'll have realised, there'd be no point in switching dummies. We're talking about a murder in this room, when we've explored every possible way of the murderer getting out or hiding inside. The second dummy, the one you discovered thrown beneath the window, wasn't any attempt to hide or get out. It was a last desperate attempt to remain undiscovered while in full view. It was the only dummy who didn't need changing *into* the outfit, because she was already wearing it. And because she, as Anthony kept reminding her, was the only one who could convincingly look like a disjointed dummy."

Clarice was fixed in nervous tension, her fingers now dug deeply into Amaryllis's arm.

David said: "Of course, the clothed dummy would've had to go out of the window, after Konrad's body. She couldn't have two clothed dummies in the room. And, when Clarice and Anthony left the room empty, she'd still have to work fast. This wasn't planned, you see. It arose from frantic necessity, taking opportunities as they arose. *Then* she'd have to strip, and clothe one of the dummies from the cupboard, and leave it where she'd been lying, dash up to the room above to hide the rug—because *she* knew the room, in spite of Konrad's show of indifference, as it was probably their meeting-place—and then rush down in time to appear in pants and bra in her doorway, which wouldn't take a second because the bra would be all she'd have left on her."

And I'd stepped over her at that window, and not realised!

Then at last Amaryllis swung her free hand vigorously, slashing Clarice's fingers from her arm. She was fierce and proud.

"He'd got no right . . . he took everything I offered him, and that was every damned thing I'd got. There wasn't anything left for me but Konrad, and then I discovered what he was going to do. Oh, damn him to hell . . . and because *she* was going to collect the insurance money, it had to be Clarice he was going away with secretly. And I'd never see him again! Oh, he was logical about it. The money, the money! All he bloody well thought of. I'd given him my life . . ."

And with Anthony as the sole reserve! With Anthony

taunting her, telling her, afterwards, that he knew she had done it, teasing her with her own ballet music. He'd as good as given her no alternative. There was no way for her to turn.

She headed for the door. David said quietly: "No."

She screamed openly at him, her face a distortion, all her misery there in that one frantic mime to the background of her scream. Then she threw herself towards the window. I could not move. David made a gesture of it, but she had the blind motivation of insanity. Maybe she reached for the rope. I don't know. She disappeared, and as she fell there was no more of her scream.

SIXTEEN

It seemed logical, George's hand being in plaster, that David should drive him home, while I followed in my Dolomite Sprint. But George sensed that I had at last sorted something out, and he insisted he could manage, his car being an automatic.

"Rubbish!" said David.

"No, it isn't. I owe you something, Dave." And he grinned at David's frown of perplexity.

So at last I got David alone. I was driving. I could feel he was uneasy.

"Say it, then," he said at last.

"You knew, didn't you David, long before the end, what she'd done."

"Guessed." He moved restlessly. "That was when George spoke about stripping the dummy from under the window, looking for a bullet. He said he couldn't find a hole in the suit. But, Elsa, if Konrad had been switching the suit from one dummy to the other it should've had at least seven bullet holes in it. It got me wondering why it hadn't."

"And so . . . that wretched reconstruction you planned, it wasn't because of the gun at all."

"Well . . ."

"No, it wasn't! You realised she'd left her outfit up in that room on the dummy. All you were doing was forcing her to dress up for the demonstration, or do something to cover up the fact that she couldn't."

"But I didn't expect *that*," he said firmly. "The fire threw me. It *could* have been somebody else, and with Anthony apparently hating her . . ."

"He loved her, you fool!"

"If you say so. Anyway, I don't suppose she intended to burn herself like she did."

"You're talking round it," I said sharply. "The point is—you told me a lie. You said it was all for the gun."

"I was going to explain."

"But you didn't!"

"I would've done, but then the fire started, and afterwards . . ." He stopped, fumbling for his pipe, embarrassed. I risked a glance.

"Afterwards?"

"Well . . . there was only you to stay the night with her, Elsa. So how could I tell you I thought she was a murderess? I mean . . ."

I screamed the car to a halt.

"You rotten devil!"

He looked at me anxiously. "But, Elsa, she only killed men. And she liked you."

"She hated me."

He reached over and ran a hand down my cheek.

"Elsa my love, when she went out of her way to show you what Anthony was like! That fight . . . it could've been at any time, anywhere. But she'd seen you were fascinated by him, that his least touch did things to you . . ."

"Oh, blast you, David."

I'd have said more, but he stopped my mouth in the most effective way there is.